ALSO BY MARIO VARGAS LLOSA

The Cubs and Other Stories

The Time of the Hero

The Green House

Captain Pantoja and the Special Service

Conversation in the Cathedral

Aunt Julia and the Scriptwriter

The War of the End of the World

The Real Life of Alejandro Mayta

The Perpetual Orgy

The Storyteller

In Praise of the Stepmother

A Fish in the Water

Death in the Andes

Making Waves

The Notebooks of Don Rigoberto

The Feast of the Goat

Letters to a Young Novelist

The Language of Passion

The Way to Paradise

The Bad Girl

Touchstones

The Dream of the Celt

The Discreet Hero

Notes on the Death of Culture

Sabers and Utopias

The Neighborhood

Harsh Times

I GIVE YOU MY SILENCE

I GIVE YOU MY SILENCE

A NOVEL

MARIO VARGAS LLOSA

TRANSLATED FROM THE SPANISH BY
ADRIAN NATHAN WEST

FARRAR, STRAUS AND GIROUX
NEW YORK

Farrar, Straus and Giroux
120 Broadway, New York 10271

EU Representative: Macmillan Publishers Ireland Ltd, 1st Floor,
The Liffey Trust Centre, 117–126 Sheriff Street Upper, Dublin 1,
D01 YC43

Printed in the United States of America
Originally published in Spanish in 2023 by Penguin Random House
Grupo Editorial, Spain, as *Le dedico mi silencio*
English translation published in the United States by Farrar, Straus
and Giroux
First American edition, 2026

Library of Congress Cataloging-in-Publication Data
Names: Vargas Llosa, Mario, 1936–2025 author | West, Adrian
Nathan translator
Title: I give you my silence : a novel / Mario Vargas Llosa ; translated
from the Spanish by Adrian Nathan West.
Other titles: Le dedico mi silencio. English
Description: First American edition. | New York : Farrar, Straus
and Giroux, 2026. | "Originally published in Spanish in 2023 by
Penguin Random House Grupo Editorial, Spain, as Le dedico mi
silencio"—Title page verso.
Identifiers: LCCN 2025038126 | ISBN 9780374616250 hardcover
Subjects: LCSH: Peru—Fiction | LCGFT: Fiction | Novels
Classification: LCC PQ8498.32.A65 L413 2026
LC record available at https://lccn.loc.gov/2025038126

www.fsgbooks.com
Follow us on social media at @fsgbooks

10 9 8 7 6 5 4 3 2

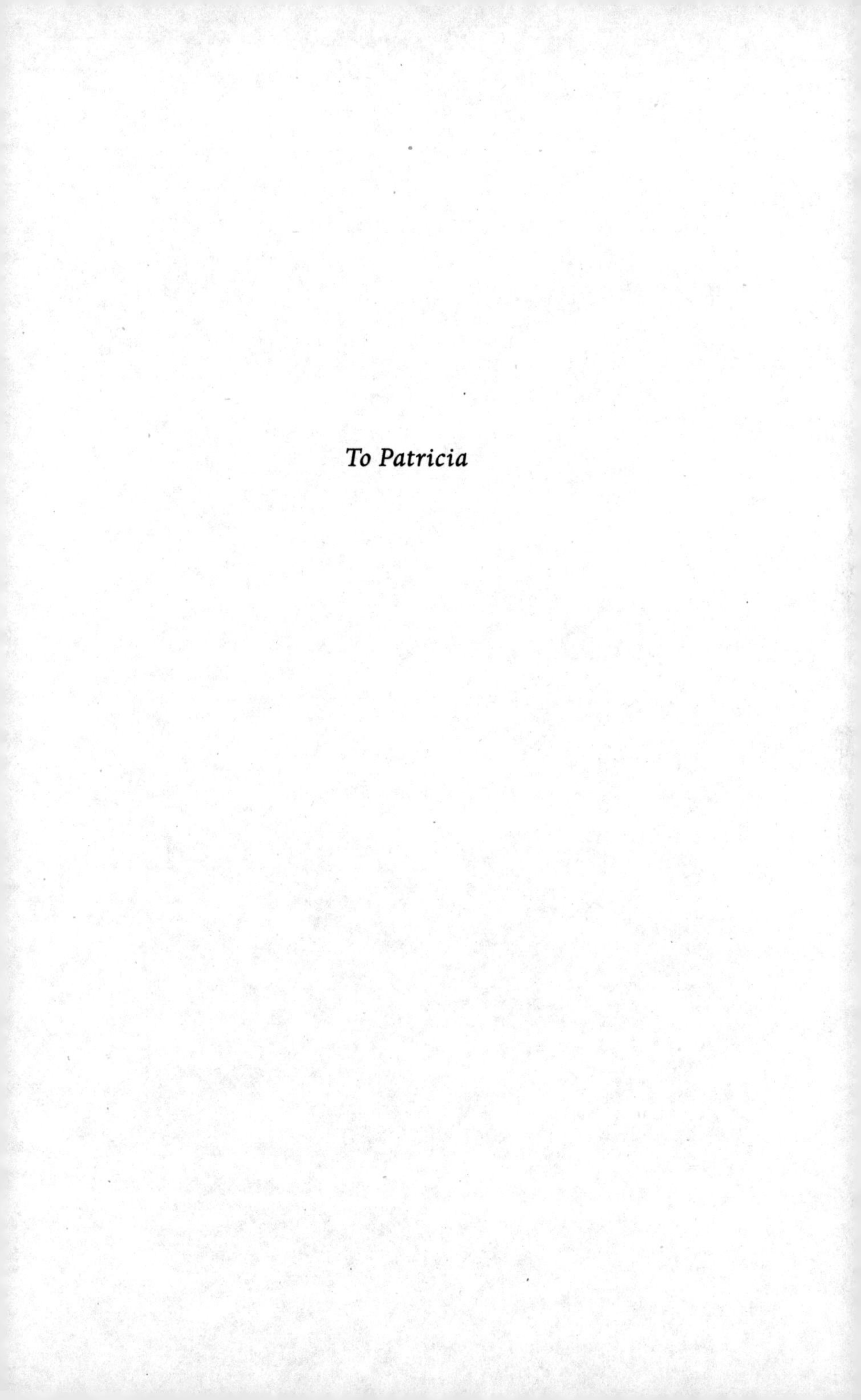

To Patricia

I GIVE YOU MY SILENCE

I

Why had José Durand Flores, that figurehead of Peru's intellectual pantheon, decided to call him? His message had reached Toño Azpilcueta through his friend Collau, who had a tavern that sold newspapers and magazines. Toño called back, but no one picked up. Collau said it was Mariquita, his daughter, who had taken the message. She was just a kid, she might have mixed up the numbers; probably he'll get back in touch, Collau said. At this point, the rats set upon Toño again: obscene little creatures that had hounded him since the early days of his childhood.

Why had José Durand Flores called? Toño didn't know him personally, but he knew who he was. A renowned writer, a man Toño at once admired and detested, one who had reached the summit and was referred to by such epithets as "illustrious man of letters" and "renowned critic," plaudits reserved for those of the country's literati who belonged, as Toño would phrase it, to the "elite." But what had he done, this José Durand Flores? He'd lived in Mexico, of course, and Alfonso Reyes, the essayist, poet, scholar, diplomat, and director of the Colegio de Mexico, had written the foreword to his celebrated anthology *Twilight of Sirens, Splendor of Manatees*, which was published there in the north. He was considered an expert on the Inca Garcilaso de la

Vega, whose library he had reassembled in his home or in the archives of some university. He was *something*, in other words, but also no big thing—really nothing, when you got down to it. Toño called again, and again he got no answer. The rodents were crawling over his body the way they did every time he felt agitated, nervous, or impatient.

Toño Azpilcueta had asked the National Library in downtown Lima to order the works of José Durand Flores, and the attendant had told him that yes, they would do so, but they never did, and so all Toño ever knew about Durand was that he was an important academic for some reason or other. If Toño had heard of him at all, this was due to a peculiar circumstance that seemed to give the lie to Durand's cosmopolitanism. Every Saturday, in the newspaper *La Prensa*, Durand published an article praising creole music and its singers, guitarists, and percussionists, people like Caitro Soto, who accompanied Chabuca Granda. This inclined Toño in his favor. Durand was contemptuous of the finicky highbrows who ignored the creole musicians utterly, sparing for them words neither of praise nor condemnation—*to hell with those people* was his attitude.

Toño Azpilcueta was a scholar of creole music—all of it, from the coastal and mountain varieties to the versions played in the Amazon. He had dedicated his life to it, and had won the distinction—naturally worthless in monetary terms—of being known as the country's greatest expert in Peruvian music, especially after the death of the grandee of Puno, Professor Hermógenes A. Morones—the *A* stood for Artajerjes, he would eventually discover. He had met Morones when he was a student at the Colegio La Salle, not long after his father, an Italian immigrant with a Basque surname, had rented the small house in La Perla where Toño would grow up. Toño earned his bachelor's degree at the National University of San Marcos, and his thesis on the Peruvian vals was overseen by Morones, whose assistant and favorite disciple he had become. Toño's work expanded upon Morones's own studies and findings concerning regional music and dance.

In his third year, the professor allowed Toño to teach several classes, and it was expected in San Marcos that, when the master retired, Toño Azpilcueta would inherit his chair. Toño took this for granted as well. For this reason, upon finishing his five years of study in the School of Arts and Letters, he began research for a doctoral dissertation to be entitled "The Street Cries of Lima," dedicated, naturally, to Morones.

From the colonial chronicles, Toño learned that town criers used to sing rather than read out announcements and municipal decrees, and their declarations reached the ears of the citizenry as a kind of music in words. With the assistance of Mrs. Rosa Mercedes Ayarza, a great specialist in Peruvian music, he learned that the cries, or *pregones*, of street vendors offering pastries, Guatemalan sponge cake, tuna, silversides, and medusafish were the oldest sounds heard on the streets of Lima. Not to mention those of the women selling *causas*, fruits, yam donuts, tamales, and tisanes.

This thought made him swell with a nostalgic pride that brought tears to his eyes. The deepest veins of the Peruvian character, that sense of belonging to a community united by tidings and proclamations, was defined by music and popular chants. This revelation would form the substance of his dissertation, which advanced steadily, in the form of abundant index cards and notebooks guarded jealously in a small suitcase, until the day Professor Morones retired and informed him with a mournful countenance that San Marcos had decided, rather than to nominate Toño as his successor, to do away with the professorship in Peruvian Studies. The courses Morones had offered were elective, and fewer and fewer students from the School of Arts and Letters attended them each year. It was this lack of participation that signaled the end.

When his dreams of a professorship were shattered, Toño Azpilcueta flew into such a rage that he was tempted to tear every index card, every notebook in his suitcase into a million pieces. Fortunately, he didn't do this, but he did abandon his plans for a dissertation. His one remaining consolation was that he had become a true scholar of popular music and dance, a "proletarian intellectual" of the country's folk traditions, as he put it. Why had Peru's music so captured his imagination? Among his ancestors, there was not a single singer or guitarist, let alone a dancer. His father, fresh off the boat from some wretched town in Italy, had worked for the railroad in the Central Mountains and had spent much of his life traveling; his mother had been constantly in and out of the hospital with one illness or another. She died at some point in his childhood, and his memories of her drew more on his father's photographs than on anything he'd experienced himself. No, nothing in his family had influenced him. He started on his own at fifteen, writing articles on the country's folk culture to translate into words the feelings the chords of creole musicians evoked within him. It didn't go badly. He sent the first article to one of those fly-by-night magazines that came out in the fifties. Entitled "My Peru," it recounted his visit, notebook in hand, to the home of the great Felipe Pinglo Alva in Cinco Esquinas. He was paid ten *soles*, which was enough to convince him that he was now the greatest expert and writer on Peruvian music and dance. He spent the money immediately on records; he spent everything he could save on records. He invested each cent that came his way in music, until his collection became famous across Lima. Radio stations and newspapers asked him to borrow albums, but as they rarely returned them, he became tight-fisted. They left him in peace after he sold off his treasure trove to buy materials to build his home in Villa El Salvador. It no longer mattered, he told himself, the music was in his blood, in his memory, and he managed to go on writing his articles, perpetuating the legacy of Hermógenes A. Morones, may he rest in peace.

Toño's passion was purely intellectual. He couldn't sing, play the guitar, or dance. This last shortcoming in particular brought him his fair share of torments in his youth. Sometimes, at the clubs or concert halls, which he attended with a little notebook in the pocket of his suit jacket, the ladies would pull him onto the dance floor, and he'd do his best for a vals or two, which was no great effort; but he strictly avoided marineras, *huainitos*, and the northern dances, the *tonderos* from Piura and the polkas. He was uncoordinated, tripped over his feet, even fell once or twice, and after this sad spectacle decided it was best to cultivate his reputation as a man who didn't know how to dance. He would remain seated, absorbed by the music, watching the motley men and women from all parts of Lima sway in fraternal embrace, certain he was right not to join them.

The Peruvian intelligentsia with their university chairs and their books from fancy publishing houses disdained him, if they even knew who he was, but Toño never felt less than them. Maybe he didn't know much about world history, maybe he wasn't up-to-date with the fashions of French philosophy, but he did know the music and the lyrics to every marinera, pasillo, and *huainito* ever written. He'd published many articles in *Mi Perú*, *La Música Peruana*, and *Folklore Nacional*, the kind of magazines that would make their debut, print two or three issues, and then vanish, often without paying his meager fee. But what was a proletarian intellectual to do? Maybe he hadn't earned the respect of figures like José Durand Flores (or maybe he had—no one could say until he called back), but the guitarists and singers looked up to him. They were starved for a bit of publicity, and for years, Toño had been happy to give it to them, as attested by the hundreds of clippings stuffed in the same suitcase where his dissertation jottings were moldering away. His articles had memorialized creole clubs like La Palizada and La Tremenda Peña, two bars in the vicinity of the Puente del Ejército in Miraflores that had now disappeared. He had gone to all the concerts there and everywhere else, all over Lima, since he was a fifteen-year-old boy, and he liked to reminisce about them and pay tribute to their importance. Now and then, a journalist writing about Lima would seek him out. "Meet me at the Bransa," Toño would say, "on the Plaza de Armas, for breakfast." That was his only vice, those breakfasts at the Bransa, and he often had to borrow money from his wife, Matilde, to pay for them.

He earned his bread giving drafting and music classes

at the Colegio del Pilar, a Catholic school for girls in Lima's Jesús María district. They didn't pay him much, but they let his two daughters, Azucena and María, ten and twelve years old, attend for free. He'd been employed there for years now. Drawing he couldn't care less about, so he devoted most of his time to music—creole music, of course—and his true task as an instructor was to instill in his charges a love for Peru's traditions. The problem was Lima with its enormous commutes. He and his daughters had to catch two minibuses to get there—just over an hour each way, if they were lucky and there were no strikes.

He had met his wife not long before building the house on the huge empty plain that would eventually become Villa El Salvador. Who'd have thought then that one day groups of militants from the Shining Path would come there trying to topple the local government and lay siege to the inhabitants, up to and including leftist leaders like María Elena Moyano, a brave woman who just a few months before, after denouncing the guerrillas' wanton fanaticism, had been brutally murdered at a local celebration. Since their arrival there, Matilde had worked as a washerwoman and seamstress, mending shirts, pants, and anything else that put food on the table. Their marriage was less one of thriving than of getting by. They'd had their good times, especially at the beginning, when Toño still believed she might share his passion for music. He'd won her by sending her acrostics that plagiarized the most ardent verses of his favorite valses; he'd thought that those words, born of the depths of the people's sensibility, would tame her heart. But soon he had to recognize that the guitar strings didn't cause her to shudder as they did him—that Felipe Pinglo Alva's velvety voice singing poems of bitter sufferings, of the fruit of unrequited love, failed to take her breath away. When he saw that the music didn't move her, that it didn't lead her to dream of a different, warmer life, when he saw that it bored her, he stopped taking her to concerts, and as the years passed, he lived his life increasingly alone, not even bothering to tell her where he went or how he spent his weekends. His outings were generally chaste: he would talk, listen to creole music, discover new voices and new players—recording their names and details about them in his little notebooks—and admire the marvelous figures of the dancing women. He didn't drink as he once had, now that he was fifty and alcohol wreaked havoc on his stomach. At most, a mini bottle of pisco or—on a wild night—of *cañazo* rum. In these settings, Toño was in his sauce: it was rare when he wasn't the most knowledgeable one in the room, and when someone posed him a question, those around would fall silent, as if he were an honored professor. He may not have published any books; his articles may have attracted little interest—and none at all among illustrious men of letters—but in those dark, echoey bars with their posters of women in veils and photos of the city's famed balconies, where the real Peru was palpable, its pure and authentic aroma, there was no one more prestigious than he.

It was one of those days when his mood was low and to lift his own spirits he was telling himself that he would finish his book on Lima's criers, get his doctorate, and find a publisher who would pay him. He repeated this thought like a mantra, and his morale slowly improved as he walked the earthen streets of Villa El Salvador. He could see his home in the distance, and in front of it Collau's bar and newsstand. After another hundred feet, he saw Mariquita, Collau's oldest daughter, coming out and walking toward him.

When she got close, he gave her a kiss on the cheek and asked her, "How are you, dear?"

"He called you again," Mariquita replied. "The same guy as yesterday."

"José Durand Flores?" he said, and took off running toward the bar, hoping nobody would hang up before he got there. When he lifted the receiver, he heard a confident voice on the line.

"You're harder to get hold of than the president himself. I am speaking with Mr. Toño Azpilcueta, correct?"

"The very same," Toño confirmed. "This is Doctor Durand Flores, no? I'm sorry I missed you yesterday. I called back, but I'm afraid Mariquita, my friend's daughter, took down the wrong number. How can I help you?"

"I'd be willing to bet that the name Lalo Molfino doesn't ring any bells for you," the man on the other end replied. "Or am I wrong?"

"No . . . Lalo Molfino, you said?"

"He's the finest guitarist in Peru. Maybe the finest in the world," Durand Flores asserted with conviction, even with a compulsive air. "I'm calling to invite you to a session this evening. Lalo will be playing. You shouldn't miss it. Write this down: the place is in Abajo el Puente, close to the Plaza de Acho. Are you free?"

"Yes, yes. Of course," Toño responded, almost alarmed that a musician of talent had escaped his notice. "Lalo Molfino . . . No, I've definitely never heard of him. I'll be happy to attend. Can you give me the exact address? And you said tonight, around nine, I assume?"

Toño Azpilcueta would go, more to see Doctor Durand Flores than to see this Lalo Molfino, with no notion that this invitation would reveal to him a truth that until then he had only intuited.

II

They are rather old structures, some dating back a century or two. The dwellings for the poor and modest folk were built piecemeal by architects or foremen, with a sheet of corrugated tin thrown on for a roof, around a courtyard where a pipe spouted water, often contaminated, and the neighbors would line up there to wash their faces and bodies if they were the cleanly sort, and to fill their bottles and buckets with water for their laundry and cooking.

It goes without saying that these famous alleyways of Lima were a breeding ground for rats. The great Peruvian creole composer Abelardo Gamarra, who signed his works "The Scoundrel," in 1907 wrote a celebrated description of the city's alleys that shows the spiritual and physical maladies occasioned by the presence of these horrible little beasts.

The oldest alleyways, those of Malambo and Monserrate, must date back to the earliest days of the colony, but most have their origins in the nineteenth century, after General José de San Martín declared the independence of the republic in 1809 and people flooded into Lima, especially the Rímac or Abajo el Puente and Barrios Altos districts. Most of those who came to the capital were poor, and it was easier to find work there than in the provinces, even if it was just as a cook, a doorman, a bodyguard, a butler. The less generous claimed that Lima's alleyways were where the wicked and disreputable of the old city gathered. They were exaggerating, if only a bit.

Nearly all the neighborhoods at the city's core, or all the oldest ones, feature these alleys: rows of small rooms lining a courtyard, rented or purchased by whole families. Parents and children and immigrants to the capital would sleep in them, sometimes on mattresses thrown on the ground or, for the slightly better off, in bunk beds two or three tiers high, which the residents occasionally built from sticks, boards, and ladders with their own hands. It's hard to imagine how these humble, pitiable dwellings could house so many people, from grandparents to great-grandparents to newborn babies. The heart of the people beat in them, but the overcrowding was brutal, and they were a breeding ground for the plagues that periodically ravaged the local population.

No one could have predicted that these alleyways would grow to be the haven of Peruvian popular music, above all the vals, which was played out in the open, with no microphone, no stage, no dance floor. *Jaranas*, these parties were called—the word must have been born with the music itself—and in the narrow rooms and on the streets, on sleepless nights when pure pisco, *cañazo* rum from the mountains, and delicious wines from the cellars of Ica ignited the people from within, they'd dance the *zamacueca*, the marinera, the vals for two days, even three—as long as the body held out. How did the alley-dwellers manage it with their precarious means? Such are the mysteries and miracles of poverty in Peru.

In those alleys were born Peru's first great guitarists and

cajon players and the masters of the vals, the *huainito*, the marinera, and the *resbalosa*. Young ladies of the moneyed classes would take dance lessons from teachers who were generally black, while couples like the famous Montes and Manrique, Salerno and Gamarra, or Medina and Carreño would light up Lima's harsh winter nights and cool down its summers, and the only things that changed were their costumes and the alcohol people toasted with. They were happy, those men and women, but they died young, often of diseases carried on the greasy coats, the grimy feet, the pestilent snouts of the rats nesting in the cracks and crevices of Barrios Altos.

They were good neighbors, those people raised in the alleyways, good friends who aided each other in sickness and in health, always ready to lend a hand, to help you get through the day, to celebrate the births of sons and daughters, to stand you a round of drinks, their companionship made more intense by the precariousness of their lives with no future. The alleyways were famous for this warmth and the ease with which it arose. Among the wealthier, there was nothing comparable. And for the seventy thousand Limans (let us call them that, even if most came from the small towns of the country's interior) who lived in the alleyways, creole music was synonymous with home.

These narrow streets lined with dwellings could be found all over the city, but the black people (the mixed-race *morenos*), many of them runaway or emancipated slaves, tended to live in Malambo with families they'd often struggled to reunite. That place, with its lusty name, hosted the most storied *jaranas*, with tap dancing, resonant singing, intricate fingerpicking, and virtuosos of the cajon, a humble wooden box invented by poor Peruvians from which the most audacious, ingenious sounds could be extracted, giving rhythmic structure to the creole valses. Felipe Pinglo Alva himself was no stranger at these parties that enlivened Lima's streets for many hours or sometimes days on end without stopping, though he always left early—"early" in this case being a manner of speaking—because he had to work the next day. And work he did; he is said to have composed three hundred pieces before his death.

This music emerged from Lima's streets, flourishing and winding its way prodigiously into the social life of the country, gaining the favor of the upper classes and seducing the salons of the rich and noble, introduced by young people bored of the antiquated music of Spain, who prized in the songs of their homeland the references to local customs and the seedier side of life. As creole music spread, the old dance teachers who made their living instructing debutantes closed up shop, preferring a change of profession to death by starvation.

Three centuries after the Spanish conquest, the music born in those narrow streets could be called authentically Peruvian, and the proud author of the present lines considers it the country's most sublime contribution to world culture. Sublime enough even to make up for Lima's rats.

Before the alleyways were built, Lima was already a city known for revelry. Its chief amusement was Carnival, or Shrovetide, when water flowed from one end of the city to the other, soaking passersby, who would stop and play with the sopping wet children in the street. Then there were the *retretas*, open-air concerts celebrating the birthday of a fiancée, a father, a brother, a friend, with multitudes and singing and guitars. These celebrations predated the famous Saint John's Eves on the hills of Amancaes. Most raucous, perhaps, was the Dance of the Devils, which the chroniclers say was very popular, though now there are no traces of it left.

What sort of city was Lima? In his agreeable 1977 book *El Waltz y el valse criollo,* César Santa Cruz Gamarra writes that a census carried out in Peru's capital in 1908 found some 140,000 inhabitants of the following characteristics (employing the language of the time): 58,683 white; 48,133 mestizo; 21,473 Indian; 6,763 black; and 5,487 yellow. In this small, mixed society, which got along despite its prejudices, the most popular instrument, according to this same source, was the harmonica, if we exclude whistling, which the citizens indulged in loudly as they ran through its streets. I say "ran" because racing was the most popular sport, one open to all members of society. Already then, the vals and the marinera had begun to replace the *zamacueca* as the public's preferred music, and were played by the military bands that would give public concerts in the town squares.

In those years, the celebrated duo of Montes and Manrique was hired by the Columbia Phonograph Company to travel to New York and record Peruvian songs. The resulting albums contained a number of *tonderos* and *resbalosas* that were praised effusively by the local press.

Peru's capital was small in those days. La Colmena, Plaza San Martín, University Park—none of these existed. And with the lack of transportation, few neighborhoods had emerged on the city's outskirts. Yet it was in Lima that the

Peruvian vals took form, and in just a few years, it would become the music of the nation and the most representative expression of its society, overtaking all rivals and weaving itself into the culture naturally, with no sanction or endorsement beyond the enthusiasm of the proud Peruvians themselves.

III

That night, after washing his face and putting on his best suit and collared shirt with his blue tie—his one truly elegant suit, the one he saved for special occasions—Toño Azpilcueta left Villa El Salvador for Abajo el Puente, Lima's old colonial district. He had been robbed there once, ten years ago. Calm, acquiescent, he had handed over his wallet, in which the robbers, to their disappointment, found a single ten-*sol* bill. Of course they made fun of him for it, and he had to return home by taxi, paying when he got there with the change he kept hidden in a blue billfold under his bed.

Since then, Toño had held Abajo el Puente, with its beggars, in low regard despite the charm of its antique architecture and of the Paseo de Aguas. "Aguas"—some name for the tubercular waters of the Rímac River, which drained from pitiful springs amid rocks and sand mounds and snaked past the Convent of Our Lady of the Angels, the houses of the wealthy, and palaces ravaged by time. Then there was the Paseo de Amancaes and the Plaza de Acho, which filled with life during the Fair of el Señor de los Milagros, with its bullfights and the music streaming from the many nearby clubs that played creole music.

It didn't take Toño long to find where the performance

was taking place, and he recognized many of those in attendance as soon as he entered. To call it a house was an understatement—it was almost a mansion, two stories high with a seemingly infinite number of rooms, one of a few older homes preserved in their original state in that neighborhood; most had been divided and subdivided into warrens. There were many people there, more than usual, men and women alike drinking shots of pisco doled out by José Durand Flores—in shirtsleeves and glasses, as Toño had seen him in photos—who was taking more than the occasional drink himself. "Cheers, brother, cheers," he would say as he knocked them back. He greeted Toño cordially when he noticed his presence, as though the two men had known each other for ages.

"Get ready for what you're about to hear, my friend. I'll tell you now, this kid Lalo, he can make those guitar strings sing like no other."

Toño attempted to respond, but though Durand Flores seemed happy that he was there, he showed no desire to engage in conversation, instead serving him a pisco, encouraging him to knock it back quickly, and turning to say hello to the other guests. Toño, cut off before he could speak, immediately regretted having come. The first groups to play he knew all too well, having tried to promote them in his own articles. He sat on a bench by a small pond with flowers and plants floating in it. He soon wearied of shaking hands and hugging all those acquaintances who approached him, tipsy after their drinks, and was about to walk off to avoid their harangues when Durand Flores emerged from the crowd, clapping his hands to quiet everyone before he spoke. He, too, had overindulged, this was evident as he informed them that this evening they were gathered to present to the public—"the distinguished public," were his exact words, and with them he was referring to the most knowledgeable connoisseurs of creole music—a young guitarist from Chiclayo whom he described as "beyond compare." He had just arrived in Lima, and was for that reason unknown, but the audience should give him a round of applause. His collaboration as the newest member of the Perú Negro ensemble, Durand Flores said, marked a new stage for the group, who would soon be taking the country's music over the border with a tour that would begin in Santiago de Chile. Durand made thc sign of the cross and said, "Repent and be silent!" And the audience obeyed.

The room went dim apart from a single spotlight. The supposed star in the making appeared. The first thing Toño noticed—and it was a detail he'd never forget—were the patent leather shoes the young man from Chiclayo wore. They were his trademark, his calling card, so to speak, worn without socks. Lalo's suit was too small, or at least the pants barely reached mid-calf. He was wearing a flowered shirt, and his hair was curled in a style rarely seen on the street in those days, long and black, with the odd streak of premature gray. His mouth opened slightly to show off two rows of very white teeth. He was rather surly and didn't speak, not even to acknowledge the scant applause that greeted him. Sitting on a chair, tuning his guitar, he turned his eyes nervously to the spectators.

When he heard the first chords, Toño finally looked away from the guitarist's shoes. And something strange happened. His irritation at Durand Flores's indifference disappeared, everything around him became a blur, and all that was left was the guitar, which that young man—a boy, in all honesty—made sigh, weep, soar, and subside before the audience in a way he had never heard before, he who had heard every professional guitarist in Peru, from the legendary to the insignificant. And that included the "first guitarist of Peru" himself, Óscar Avilés, the big man with the pencil-thin mustache.

The silence that overtook those listening in the garden of that enormous house struck Toño as like the silence of a bullring—the same silence he remembered, the same silence he would never forget, on that Sunday afternoon in 1956 or '57 in the Plaza de Acho, during the fair, when his father had taken him to see the bulls fight for the first time, telling him that Procuna, the Mexican toreador, was hit-or-miss, a man of extremes. One day, he might fall prey to fear and run shamelessly from the horned beasts, letting the flagmen and lancers do his dirty work; on another occasion, he would swell with bravery and artistry and overtake the animal with such grace and agility that he'd make the watchers in the front rows swoon.

Since that day in his tender boyhood, he'd had a taste for the bullring, and had gone back almost every year, but never again had he heard that deep, ecstatic silence, felt that expectancy that made you too timid to draw a breath or even think, that sucked every thought from your head as you watched, rapt, drunken, immobile, waiting for the miracle to occur, as Procuna, the very essence of elegance, courage, and wisdom, made a right-hand pass, drew the cape straight across the bull's nose, stepped closer and closer to the beast, became one with him in a single instance of refinement. But there it was again now, that silence, sacred, elemental, primordial, as the boy from Chiclayo strummed, wringing profound, disconcerting, unprecedented tones from the strings that had a ring of madness that rendered the silence around Toño tangible. Everyone there, man and woman, young and old, had forgotten their earlier laughter and chit-chat, the jokes, the compliments, the claps on the back, and was listening, rapt, hypnotized, as the strings trembled in the midst of the formidable stillness that had overtaken the night.

He had heard that such reverential silence sometimes fell over the bullring in Seville or in Las Ventas in Madrid, but he had known it only once and was shocked to hear it again, provoked by a mestizo boy from Chiclayo sitting a few steps away. He was playing a vals, but one Toño didn't recognize because those strings, submissive to Lalo Molfino's miraculous fingering, issued a sound like nothing he had ever heard. It was as if the music were penetrating him, entering his body, marrying with his blood and flowing through his veins. Too bad for poor Óscar Avilés—the "first guitarist of Peru" was first no more.

It wasn't just his skill as his fingers danced over the frets, playing notes that sounded as though they'd been invented on the spot. It was something more: wisdom, concentration, and discipline, talent, sure, but also something miraculous. Something that left the audience dumbstruck. Tears bathed Toño's face, his soul opened wide with longing, and he longed to embrace his countrymen, his brothers and sisters, who had witnessed this marvel. And he wasn't alone. Even Durand Flores had taken out his handkerchief. Toño wanted to walk over to him, to hug him. "My kinsman," he whispered, feeling that the same blood must run in their veins. So deeply had the music permeated those present that any social, racial, intellectual, or political differences between them faded into the background. An electric wave of fellow feeling, love, benevolence swept over the garden. Toño was certain no one had been immune to it. And when Lalo Molfino rose, very thin, standing very straight, indifferent to the ovation as he held his guitar, Toño couldn't help but see in the spectators' smiles, their glimmering eyes, their reddened cheeks, the signs of fraternal love and love of country.

The boy from Chiclayo bowed slightly and disappeared into one of the house's many hallways. But the applause didn't die, even as occasional words filtered through it. The audience was enchanted, and Toño Azpilcueta felt the urge to shake the hand of that wizard, to ask him a few questions. But look as he might, ask around as he might, no one could tell him where Molfino had gone. Durand Flores had turned merrily back to his guests and was once more filling their glasses with pisco. As they toasted, he spoke over and over of the revival of Perú Negro and their imminent departure for Santiago. Toño Azpilcueta hugged him and wished him the best of luck in his travels. "You'll teach those Chileans what the real Peru is all about," he said, flushed, and exited the courtyard of that house in Abajo el Puente that he would never forget. He was in a good mood as he returned home, thinking of the article that he would write that same night, or, better, in the morning, at the National Library in the center of town, right on the Avenida Abancay. He already had a title: "Silence Falls Under the Bridge."

That night, for once, the rats and other vermin didn't creep into his dreams and wake him. Before he fell asleep, he looked up at the ceiling of his home, still inflamed from experiencing Lalo Molfino's playing. Matilde was sleeping next to him, mouth open, tossing and turning, as she did every night. He looked at her and thought for a moment that she was as pretty as Cecilia Barraza. He wanted to wake her, give her kisses on the cheek and neck, make love to her impulsively as they had in the old days, but Matilde didn't respond to his entreaties. Groggy, she slapped him away like a rag doll and turned onto her other side. Toño didn't let it embitter him. He had heard Lalo Molfino, after all. His dreams would be sweet, and tomorrow he would write the best article of his entire life.

IV

No sooner had the creole vals appeared—and this says something about how quickly it spread through all the social classes in Peru—than young men of good breeding and bad habits began to frequent the alleyways in the working-class neighborhoods where valses played and parties went on for days on end with abundant singing and dancing. It goes without saying they stopped in the brothels, too; some even fell in love with the girls. There were fights between the old residents of the neighborhoods and these new arrivals. The latter formed a fraternity that came to be known as La Palizada, a reference to the flooding rivers of the Peruvian Amazon, which would swell and roar and level everything in their path. Its members were known as *faites*, from the English "fighters," for obvious reasons.

Abelardo Gamarra, the Scoundrel, a master journalist and lover of creole culture, cared little for La Palizada and its *faites*, a type whom he defined thusly: "the handsome young fellow who claims he has no fear, not even of the devil himself; or the charmer who truly has no fear. The *faite* deems himself a leader or chief and imposes his will by force." Of La Palizada's members, he writes: "They had no object other than entertainment, carousal, imbibing, settling scores with their fists, squandering all they could, all their families could afford, selling off their fathers' shirts or their mothers' petticoats if they had to . . . They fought with brio, butted heads, threw haymakers that hit like lead, and they'd single out the biggest, handsomest of their rivals for a swift kick that would leave him trotting away on bandy legs."

The Scoundrel also relates how La Palizada moved into politics and began buying off powerful people, but someone who should know—a member of the fraternity, Toni Lagarde, incidentally a dear friend of the author of these lines—assures me that this was untrue, and that the group's members kept a strict distance from the country's political life.

What they did do was fight boldly, ferociously, when needed, fired by their dawning manhood. One of their main leaders was Alejandro Ayarza, the brother of Rosa Mercedes Ayarza de Morales, an author, a composer of valses, and a lady of distinguished character whom the scholar Eduardo Mazzini calls "our great compiler of popular songs." His opinion is seconded by another expert in the Peruvian vals, Manuel Zanutelli.

This Alejandro Ayarza, who was better known by the pseudonym Karamanduka, apart from leading his band of wayward rascals, wrote a vals of his own entitled "La Palizada," which Mazzini and Zanutelli agree perfectly defines the essence of that group:

> Who hasn't heard of us young men
> In this old and noble town?
> We stride with grace through tavern doors
> And every man stands down.

We are the lords of the dance floor
And we make the cajon sing,
And when it's time to rumble,
We're happy to do our thing.

Give me the ducats, ducats, ducats,
Give me the ducats, the dark girls say,
Give me the ducats, ducats, ducats,
But Karamanduka says no way.

Bring cups of healthy liquor,
Bring cups not watered down,
Bring cups of Peruvian liquor,
Line them up and we'll drink them down.

Long live the men who are brave as beasts,
Long live money, love be blessed,
Long live ladies, long live feasts,
Long live the liquor that warms our breast.

Give me the ducats, ducats, ducats . . .

From the ranches every sundown
To Puerto Arturo I make my way,
Where Don Silverio comes down
With fine tobacco for our soiree.

And we spend our nights content,
The cajon rumbles, the guitars strum

As we drown our laments
In the vapors of the finest rum.

Give me the ducats, ducats, ducats . . .

We don't know the meaning of labor,
We party, flirt, and fight,
On the floor cutting capers
And singing to our heart's delight.

La Palizada, that's our name,
The sharpest group around.
La Palizada, we earned our fame
As the toughest boys in town.

Give me the ducats, ducats, ducats . . .

Allegedly, these lyrics occurred to Karamanduka one night when he and other members of La Palizada were in jail, probably because some party or other they'd attended had ended in a brawl, as was typical with the spirited young men of Peru in general, whelps of a nation fed on the purest patriotic sentiments. It's said that when Karamanduka pleaded with the officer in charge to free them, he promised to do so if he could compose a fine vals, with lyrics, on the spot. Karamanduka took him up on this, composing "La Palizada" in a few precious minutes.

"La Palizada" was, for those restless young men, a ticket to freedom. In these pages, I will tell the story of the romance that blossomed between one of them, Toni Lagarde, and Lala, muse of the alleys of Barrios Altos. Their union and undying love is the empirical proof of a thesis to be put forth in the present work.

As the peculiar form of waltz native to Peru spread across the country, marking a high point for creole music that would never be surpassed—one that remains influential even today—La Palizada spread, too. Gonzalo Toledo, in one of his chronicles for *El Comercio*, writes that in the beautiful town of Huancayo, washed by the waters of the Mantaro River, there was a Palizada Huanca, named for the indigenous culture that flourished in the region before the arrival of the Incas. Its members included doctors, lawyers, and public servants, who were presumably more civil than their Liman counterparts.

It was on the streets of Lima's old town, trying to scout the most renowned alleyways—those most closely associated with creole music—that I had my nastiest encounter with its rats. My beloved Lima, we must admit, suffers from this defect, one shared by all the great old cities, even Paris, which over the centuries has bred millions of rats beneath its streets. I found myself in Malambo, the famous black quarter, sniffing around in an ancient alleyway in utter dereliction, when I felt something fall on my right shoulder from the collapsed roof of the house I had entered. Assuming it was a chunk of brick, I flicked it away without looking, but it stayed there, feeling heavy, and I turned my head to see what it was. My heart froze for a few moments as I saw, lying flat on my shoulder, still frightened by the blow I had given it, a nasty, chubby rat staring at me with its little crossed eyes. Struggling to breathe, I hit it again and it fell to the floor, stunned—perhaps even more so than I—for a few seconds before running and hiding amid the rubbish littering the ground.

Such are the blemishes great countries must bear, and Peru is no different. Rats bring corruption, illness, and debility, and undermine the collective spirit music has forged. To put an end to these beasts is less an aesthetic question than a moral priority. I appeal to the good judgment of the competent authorities in this regard.

V

Several months had passed since that night in Abajo el Puente, and Toño Azpilcueta had heard nothing more of Lalo Molfino. He thought the music press would report on Perú Negro's tour in Chile, but time passed and he saw nothing, though every week he went punctually to the kiosk and waited for the magazines to arrive so he could page through them. He heard a rumor that the kid from Chiclayo had left Perú Negro and was now playing with Cecilia Barraza, so he asked her to meet with him at his beloved Bransa, where he was flush enough to treat himself to breakfast. The mere thought of her made his heart race. He was nervous, expectant, the way he always was when he saw Cecilia, and for that reason, he failed to notice Doctor José Durand Flores as he approached his table, in glasses, a tie, and a snug suit. He looked huge and ill at ease as he reached out his hand.

"Are you all alone?" he asked. "If so, would you mind if I sit with you?"

"I'd be honored," Toño said, standing up and bowing slightly. "I owe you a debt of gratitude, one I'm afraid I'd struggle to repay. You're the one who invited me to that magnificent night of music in the company of Lalo Molfino."

Durand Flores sighed and fell into a chair that creaked under his weight.

"You know, the cheese buns here are exquisite," he said, shaking his head slightly, as if he wished to hear nothing of that night at the club, of Lalo Molfino, or of anything that had happened since. When the waiter came, he ordered the specialty he'd mentioned, along with a large café con leche.

"I used to drink hot chocolate," he said, still looking displeased, "but the only good chocolate in Peru is from Cuzco, and it's almost impossible to find."

Toño ignored this remark and returned to the subject that interested him, Lalo Molfino and his tour in Chile. How had they reacted, those poor people who weren't fortunate enough to be born in Peru? Did they bow down and praise Lalo's talents? Had his guitar cooled their fiery Mapuche blood? Durand Flores told him curtly that it had been a fiasco. Perú Negro was done for, and that was all he cared to say about it.

"Wednesday I'll be going to Paris, and there I'll taste chocolate again. And I hope I won't have to return to Lima for a long time. Or to Peru, for that matter."

He uttered these words with a repugnance that took Toño aback. Not wanting to worsen matters, he waited a moment, then said succinctly, "I just wanted you to know I haven't forgotten that night in Abajo el Puente. Thanks to you, and thanks to Lalo's playing. I can't get it out of my head. I'd have called to express my gratitude, but I didn't know how."

The café con leche had arrived, and the buns with mountain cheese, and Durand Flores looked at them, nodding. He was a chubby man, not fat, with a soft, friendly voice that put one at ease.

Toño couldn't stop himself from adding, "I hope you read my article in *Folklore Nacional*."

"I didn't, I never saw it," Durand Flores said, preparing to take a second bite of the bun he had already started on. "I've tried to forget everything about that night."

"Not I. I'll remember it forever. I've got little doubt but that listening to Lalo was the most enriching musical experience I've ever known. And that was the last I heard of him. I might have hoped for a letter of thanks after my enthusiastic response to his concert."

"I can promise you he never read it," Durand Flores replied. "I don't think Lalo could read. He died, didn't you know? Some say it was suicide."

Toño felt as though his heart had stopped, as though the world were closing around him. Lalo Molfino, dead? A suicide? He could have cried then and there, but he opened his eyes wide to stanch the flow of tears. He was a weeper. That and his horror of rats were his two great weaknesses. José Durand Flores, meanwhile, chewed his buns with relish, taking great sips from his mug of café con leche.

"He was a strange boy," Durand continued, not bothering to swallow first. "I hired him because of the way he worked the frets. But in Chile, he gave us headache after headache. He avoided everyone, refused to go out with the group, always wanted to play solo. A nightmare, I tell you. The guys hated him, they thought he looked down on them because he was mestizo and they were black; you know how these things go. It went beyond that, though. He barely understood that other people even existed. Lalo Molfino was as vain as they come. He thought he was the best guitarist in Peru. Of course, he was, wasn't he?"

"If you asked me, sir, I'd say yes," Toño responded, unable to accept that the thin mestizo with the patent leather shoes was dead. "So you say it was suicide?"

"I'm pretty sure it was tuberculosis, actually. His lungs were eaten through. And he had other illnesses, too. He never ate, you could see that yourself from how thin he was. But the talk around Lima was that he killed himself. I wasn't around at the time—I was in Santiago trying to pay down our debts. We lost every cent we invested in Perú Negro. It was an outright disaster. For me and for my partners."

Toño peppered him with more questions, but Durand Flores, reluctant to answer, told him, "Look, I don't know much, just that he died here in Lima not long after returning from Chile. They say it was sudden, he was at the Hospital Obrero, it's a miracle they even took him in. It's a shame, right? A hell of a loss."

Having finished his meal, Durand Flores raised his hand to ask the waiter for the check.

"Are you really leaving?" Toño asked, his hunger stirred by the lingering aroma of the buns and mountain cheese.

"I fly out Wednesday, as I told you. I'm counting the hours."

"You'll be sorely missed in Peru," Toño said and, after a moment's hesitation, moved from regret to reproach: "If I'm to be honest, I don't know what it is about France that exerts such a pull on this country's intellectuals. What do the Frogs have to teach us? Remember César Moro, he ran away there and they sent him back to us light in his loafers. And I doubt he's the only one. You ship a Peruvian over there, he comes back thinking he's better than the rest of us, and all he can do is malign his home country."

Durand Flores seemed to be choking or laughing or both things at once. But his only response was to throw a few banknotes on the table and extend his hand to Toño.

"Enjoy your morning, my friend."

"And you have a good trip, doctor," Toño said, solemn once more. "I trust I'll see you as soon as you return to your fatherland. We've lost Lalo Molfino. Let's not lose you as well."

Toño watched the big man leave the Bransa, in a hurry as always, looking pleased after devouring his breakfast. The same could not be said of Toño. He thought once more of Molfino, dead, perhaps by his own hand, and he realized glumly that he would have nightmares about rats that night. Humanity had lost one of those talents that justified its presence on this earth. And with this grim news, what was the point of waiting for Cecilia Barraza? He had asked to interview her only because he'd heard, in his efforts to track down Lalo, that Cecilia had fired him from her group after learning that he was in love with her. Was this true, or was it just gossip? It no longer really mattered. And so he would just apologize for making her rise so early and try to forget about the guitarist once and for all.

Half an hour later, when Cecilia Barraza entered the Bransa, Toño was still there at his table, still pensive, still mournful, still hearing the notes of that spirited guitar, the absence of which had now turned his life upside down. The sight of Cecilia lifted his mood slightly. She was his one true friend in the world of creole music, or at least he liked to believe she was. He had been in love with her for ages, though he'd never so much as offered her a compliment. He had kept his feelings buried in the depths of his heart, convinced that she was too good for him, too far outside his reach. He had written articles about her, one after another, praising her to high heaven, never failing to mention her elegance, the refinement of her voice, her dress, her delicacy as she strolled across the stage. He still had her records, and he listened to them as if in a trance, always alone, because Cecilia was the creole singer Matilde hated most.

"Why are you so pale, Toño?" she asked. "You look on the verge of fainting."

"Pepe Durand was just here having breakfast. He gave me some awful news. And you're right, it did make me a little faint. He said that Lalo Molfino died."

"You didn't know?" Cecilia asked.

She looked distinguished in her thin shawl, her high leather boots, and her raincoat, with a matching clutch under her arm. Her makeup was exquisite. She must have just showered, and her lively, scintillating eyes looked beautiful as she settled down in the chair next to him. Noticing her newly manicured hands, he imagined, in a stupor, how happy he would have been married to a woman like her. But then his thoughts turned somber once more. Lalo Molfino, dead. He still couldn't believe it.

"I asked you here because I wanted to talk about him," Toño said. "But now, what's the point, right? Is it true that he was in love with you?"

"That's what people said," she replied with a smile, not giving the rumors much weight. She kept her voice soft so the people at the neighboring table wouldn't hear her. "But he never mentioned it to me. Lalo was timid. Maybe he couldn't bring himself to do it. He never flirted, never dropped any hints, and for two months or so, we were around each other constantly. You can't imagine what a headache he was."

"You knew him well, then," Toño concluded, deciding to take another sip of his chamomile tea, which was ice cold, as he'd expected. Cecilia had ordered, as always, tea with lemon and a bottle of mineral water.

"He had great gifts, you know," she said. "But he was also vain, smug, incredibly difficult. A neurotic the likes of which I've never seen. He refused to play with the rest of the band, he wanted the stage for himself alone. The whole company hated him. They called him 'the one and only.' He never talked to them, and everyone thought he looked down on them. Of course, he played the guitar like a dream. But if I hadn't fired him, the whole company would have quit on me. That last day, when he came to say goodbye, was the only time I ever saw him sad. 'I give you my silence,' he said, and departed, almost ran off. I don't know what he meant by that: *I give you my silence.* Does that mean anything to you?"

"When I heard him playing at Abajo el Puente, a silence fell like you hear at times in the bullring," Toño said. "It touches my soul, him having said that. *I give you my silence.* Of course he was in love with you, Cecilia."

Toño observed her. She still looked very young. He remembered when El Negro Ferrando discovered her on his show on Radio América when she was a little girl, with that sweet little voice and those eyes . . . How many times had Toño interviewed her, or written about her, singing her praises? Dozens, maybe hundreds. He didn't regret it. She never disappointed her admirers.

Toño confessed, "I asked you here because I was looking

to get in touch with Lalo." He shrugged. "I was hoping to meet him, maybe for an interview. Poor kid. What Durand Flores said crushed me, and now I'm unsure what to do. I don't suppose it makes much sense to go on researching him."

"Well, now, I can tell you a few things about him," Cecilia said, opening and closing her glimmering eyes. "He was a guitarist of genius, but a very strange sort of genius. He never went out, you know. Never saw the sights with the rest of us, never went to see the places we were going to play beforehand. We were in Ica, in Arequipa, in Puno, in Cuzco. We spent lots of time out and about. Not him. He never even saw Lake Titicaca. He'd shut himself up in his room with his guitar, tuning it, changing the strings. He'd spend the whole day in there. I swear I'm telling the truth, you can choose whether or not to believe me. None of the tourist stuff interested him, none of the people. All that mattered to him in this life was his guitar. Turning the pegs, polishing the body, waxing the neck. He lived for that thing."

"You thought he was a genius, but you threw him out," Toño said.

"He never got along with anybody. The other musicians couldn't stand him. They knew he was talented, of course, but they thought he had a screw loose. I'm not so sure. Maybe he really was that way, maybe it was a pose."

"How did you find out he'd died?"

"Someone told me. He was gravely ill, they said, laid up in the Hospital Obrero. So I went to see him."

He was in a ravaged state, Cecilia said, and she barely recognized him lying there in the infirmary with dozens of the sick and dying. The doctor told Cecilia not to touch him, and absolutely not to kiss him: he was consumed by tuberculosis and wouldn't last much longer. He would die there without any family to comfort him—the hospital could find no next of kin. She went to the edge of his bed. His eyes were closed, and remained that way the whole time she stood there.

"He'd always been skinny," Cecilia said. "But it was much worse . . . He was skin and bones and nothing more. He seemed to be sleeping, or maybe he just didn't want to talk to anyone. I went back a few days later, but he'd already died. Since there was no one to claim the body, they buried him in a common grave."

Toño found this hard to believe, a scandal, and as despair burned in his breast, he told himself his nightmares that evening would be far worse than usual.

"That's what they told me anyway. I didn't ask many questions. Apparently that's what they do there when nobody lays claim to the remains. Poor guy. He was a mystery. He might not have had any family. He was from Chiclayo, supposedly."

"That much is true," Toño replied. "I mean, he wasn't from the city. He was from the outskirts, from Puerto Etén, I think."

They both fell silent for a while, Toño because he was afraid if he spoke, his voice would crack and he would make a scene in front of her. That urge to cry wouldn't leave him—and over a person he'd never spoken a word to in his life! In that moment, he made a decision. Come hell or high water, he would write a book about Lalo Molfino. He would comb through the newspapers and magazines, would talk with all the people who had known him. This book would be an homage to his talent, but also much more: he would at last put to paper those ideas about the Peruvian vals he had entertained so often as he'd observed the effect the music had on its public, epitomized in Lalo's concert in Abajo el Puente. He would write the book even if he couldn't find a publisher, make it known that the greatest guitarist in the world had been born here in Peru. His heart was beating faster than usual—that was Cecilia's presence—and it gave him courage. Her scent was delicate like fresh water, but fragrant. She was smiling, beautiful, graceful, as always. He imagined the guitarist's body lying in a potter's field, and it infuriated him to his depths. Not even the death of Hermógenes A. Morones had affected him so. At the latter's wake, the crowd was teeming, and even the president of the republic had sent a wreath. But now, Lalo was forgotten. It wasn't fair. Toño would write his book about Peruvian music, even if he had to pay from his own pocket to publish it, and he was sure he would make it a fitting homage to Lalo and a contribution toward solving the great problems that plagued the nation.

VI

No one knows when it became the custom for the citizens of Lima to dance and sing and spend the day in lazy entertainment on the Pampa de Amancaes. All that's certain is that in the early days, it was a religious holiday celebrated each year on June 24. Pancho Fierro's watercolors attest to its age—150 years, at any rate—and show how the city dwellers would come out on that day to bury the Carnival King who had presided over the previous festivities. Allegedly, Father Bernabé Cobo devoted a chapter of his 1653 *History of the New World* to the motley persons who would invade the pampas in his day. Historian Raúl Porras Barrenechea claims to have discovered the origin of this procession in the legend of a hermit who died with a saint's honors. But others say a wealthy miner from Potosí, Antonio Cinteros, built a chapel in Amancaes devoted to Saint John Lateran, where the saint's day was celebrated and members were initiated into the Knights Templar.

None of this is certain, however, and the most fantastical origin tales continue to surround these festivities. What matters is that when the amancae, that strange yellow flower, came into bloom, the residents of Lima, from the poshest to thc poorest, would set forth on the pampa with their instruments, settle down, and begin to play music. Children and dogs would frolic, riders would bring out their mounts, and sometimes they would even make the horses dance. Parents would watch as their daughters fell in love. And here, most likely, the Peruvian vals was born, just as it appears in the first photos ever taken in Lima.

Accounts from the time agree: from the fussiest whites to the barefoot mestizos who were slowly forgetting their Quechua and muttering in broken Spanish to the Chinese, the Japanese, the Castilians and other foreigners, all could be found on the pampa, and all languages could be heard. The old guitarists always traveled there, the forefathers of the vals, José Ayarza and Gómez Flores, Pedro Fernández and Luis A. Molina—the illustrious Old Guard, as Felipe Pinglo Alva's generation was known—and Rosa Mercedes Ayarza de Morales, who collected dozens or perhaps hundreds of Peru's songs and made them famous on the stage of the Teatro Politeama. Little children learned from their elders there how to perform the Devil's Dance—which has been lost to time, probably forever—how to play the guitar, the harmonica, the vihuela, or how to ride the young colts that would race there amid the multitude.

Don Pedro Bocanegra was famous for the serenades he crooned there for half of Lima. He was a frequent presence at the birthdays of old men and little girls. His hardy voice announced his presence in the streets, and everyone would greet him as an illustrious representative of the Old Guard. The somber strumming of his guitar opened doors for him, and crowds gathered to hear his rugged timbre. At dawn, Don Pedro would return to his room on the Callejón del Pino, known before as the Calle Patos, after surviving yet another "bohemian night," as he'd say.

Everyone respected him when he appeared in the processions at Amancaes. Him and many others like him.

Serenades were a frequent occurrence on the pampa. Young men would sing the praises of their beloved, trying to earn the regard of the better families, which were deeply and severely Catholic at the time, their lives devoted almost entirely to christenings and mourning, to burials and processions. The girls were naturally proud of these serenades, which could go on for hours or even days.

In old photos, illustrious figures like Juan Francisco Ezeta and Pedro Fernández can be seen in the dwellings of the poor, who would perform the Devil's Dance in bare feet. Some said they were portraying the devils escaping the cemetery—in other words, fleeing from hell—while others claimed the intention was to chase the evil spirits back to the underworld, so they would rot there until the end of time. This ominous religious note was uncharacteristic for this jubilant celebration, which even the presidents of the republic were known to attend. Families made great preparations beforehand, ironing their clothes, darning their dresses and suits, mixing refreshments and cooking abundant food for the two or three days they would spend in the hills, close to the clouds, where the yellow flowers would rain down over the faces of children and gentlemen.

The Pampa de Amancaes was long dead and buried by the time Chabuca Granda composed those lovely valses that commemorated it all over the globe. The city had grown, new buildings had crowded in, and there was ever less space for singing and dancing.

Today, Amancaes is more an idea than a reality: a notion of conviviality, of brotherhood uniting Limans of all classes, races, and colors, people who went there for diversion and delight, forgetting their prejudices, loving their neighbors, giving rise, on mysterious afternoons of music and glee, to that magical dance, the Peruvian vals, invention of no one and property of none.

Fights were few on the Pampa de Amancaes: if there were a brawl, a dust-up, even an argument, the adversaries were quickly separated, and friendly words stilled the hostilities. All were as one, then, and in some sense, all loved each other. And that was Peru.

Later, with the popularity of Chabuca Granda's polkas and valses, the government and the people wished to bring the good times back, with appeals to old glories like the guitarists Alcides Carreña and Alberto Condemarín. But there was no space anymore. The city had grown and the pampa had shrunk until it became what it is now, a small park drowning amid parking lots and buildings. Construction dust covers the birthplace of the Peruvian vals, that bond of music that transcended enmities to forge a connection between all the people born of this land—a connection we dream of today. This is my conviction, one I will believe in until someone shows me otherwise.

VII

Toño Azpilcueta knew he would enjoy the immense expanses of sand on the Peruvian coast, stretching north and south of Lima. The ones he saw now, as a bus owned by the Roggero company took him from Lima to Chiclayo. He hadn't traveled much in Peru, only to Cuzco and to Trujillo by plane, after being invited by the Freedom Club and by Guillermo Ganoza, that jovial local dignitary, to join the jury of the latter city's Marinera Festival, which had grown to be an enormous success since its founding in 1960.

That pale yellow sand, tending grayish at times, with its high dunes and flat planes, was a revelation to him. To the left was the foamy sea, to the right, like flying buttresses, the Andes, which he had imagined many times, drawing on the photos he'd seen and the history books he'd read and reread. The shore stretched on toward the ancient adobe city of Chan Chan, on the outskirts of Trujillo, where Peruvians once buried their dead. For a thousand years, the bones of men and animals lay there, loincloths, figurines, knotted cords, an entire exquisite society utterly different from the monumentality of the great cultures of the hills: warring people, conquerors—first the Aimara and then the Inca—who had no time for weaving the sumptuous birdwing cloaks of the coastal Paracas culture, items destined for pleasure and contemplation. Toño did not weary of observing the beaches with their choppy waves that seemed to wish to devour the rocks along the foothills.

He was happy. For days, he hadn't struggled with nightmares or visitations from rats, and thanks to a loan from his friend Collau, he had finally undertaken his trip to Chiclayo and Puerto Etén. One morning, after many nights of listening to Toño's account of the sad, brief life of Lalo Molfino, Collau had shown up at his door looking haggard and hesitant, one hand in his pocket.

"I've come to do you a good deed," Collau said. Collau was Chinese, and Toño assumed they were the same age, but it was hard to know how old or young the Chinese were, and Collau was no exception to the rule.

"Good talk last night," said Toño Azpilcueta, remembering. He hadn't been able to shut up about the guitarist, the high life in Lima, all sorts of other things. "I overdid it, maybe, once I turned to the Incas and Tahuantinsuyo. Isn't that right, compadre?"

"You said it. I thought you'd never pipe down," Collau agreed in a very thin voice. "And then it took me forever to fall asleep. I kept thinking about what you'd said. That got to me, compadre. The whole sad story about that kid. Him being in love with Cecilia Barraza, maybe. And it was so pretty, what he said when he left: *I give you my silence.*"

"I can't talk about Lalo Molfino without tears coming to my eyes, he just gets to me," Toño responded, clapping Collau on the back. "So what is this good deed you were telling me about?"

They'd been friends since the two of them built their homes with their own hands in the same neighborhood many years before, when it was under the mayorship of a long-suffering Spaniard named Michel Azcueta, an adopted son of Peru and a man like no other. There were no land titles then, but if the mayor gave his word, that was as good as gold. Toño and Collau liked to stay up late talking. Collau's wife and the mother of his three children, Gertrudis, a mountain girl from Ayacucho, didn't usually join them. Now and then, she'd come outside, give them a surly look, then go back into the house without saying a word.

"I'm going to lend you five thousand *soles*, my friend," Collau said uncomfortably, looking away, almost muttering. "So you can write that book of yours about Lalo Molfino and Peru and all that. You can go to Chiclayo and find out more about the kid's life. If you tell others what you told me yesterday, you'll bring tears to a lot of people's eyes. You saw your wife, she was crying, too."

Toño didn't know what to say. What was happening with Collau? He'd known him for years, and he'd never done anything like this.

"I'm letting you have the money because of those tears, compadre. How they came to me when I was in bed. Weird, right? I'm not a sentimental guy. But what you said about this skinny guy lying on his deathbed in the Hospital Obrero, about how great he was . . . I don't know, it just got to me," Collau said.

Dumbstruck, Toño could see Chiclayo and Puerto Etén in his mind, and thought about the questions about Lalo Molfino's childhood that needed to be answered and all the people he should interview. This would be his first book and his last; it would take him months to write, if not years. He felt a knot in his throat as Collau smiled.

"Is that a yes or a no?" he heard him say. Collau leaned into him. "It's a loan, compadre. Will you take it? Because this silence of yours, I'm not sure what it means. If you're worried about it, Gertrudis agrees. My wife is a little standoffish, Toño, but she's got an emotional side to her, like all the girls from Ayacucho."

"I just didn't expect this generosity, Collau. I'm worried you didn't hear yourself correctly. You do know that you said you'd lend me five thousand *soles*?"

"Of course." Collau nodded. He removed his hand from his pants pocket and put down a pile of banknotes. "There it is, my friend. I hope you can make all of Peru cry the way you did Matilde and me."

Toño's unbridled passion as he spoke of Lalo Molfino had infected Collau. That notion of the importance of creole music in bringing Peru together hadn't just touched his heart, Collau told Toño; it had given him the sense that he could be a part of something that would bring dignity to the people of Peru. He wasn't sentimental like the creoles who frequented the music halls, but it had moved him to hear Toño say, with a conviction bordering on exaltation, that *huachafería* and the *vals criollo* were Peru's two great contributions to world culture. It was a beautiful notion, one deserving of a book, he thought, and if he couldn't write it himself, he could lend his life savings to someone who would.

"I've never seen this much cash in one place," Toño said as he counted the bills. "I can't believe it, still. Are you sure, though, brother? I have no idea when I could pay it back."

"Don't worry about that." Collau laughed. "There's no deadline. You'll get around to it when you get around to it, and if you don't, that's all right, too. Just don't lose it, and write your book, Toño, for the love of God."

Later, Toño would tell Matilde, "Funny choice of words, because I think he just convinced me of the existence of God and heaven. God because my prayers came true, and heaven because Collau deserves to go there after doing me this favor."

He could hardly talk—could hardly express the happiness he felt.

Thanks to Collau, Toño would soon be in Puerto Etén. He had confirmed that Lalo Molfino had been born there and not in Chiclayo, and had spent his childhood in this tiny port town of some two or three thousand souls, probably learning the secrets of the guitar there. Who had his teacher been? He must have had one, and finding out would be the starting point of Toño's research.

He knew no one in this hamlet where, in better days, trains had come to from the mountains and surrounding villages. Lalo's name had to be familiar, though. Toño supposed that his time in Puerto Etén had been the most important chapter in the town's history. He would mention the guitarist, the people there would welcome him with open arms, and hundreds of friends, acquaintances, and family members would furnish him with all the information he needed. Two or three days would suffice to note it all down, and Toño could return home.

Toño had tried unsuccessfully to reserve a bus from Chiclayo to Puerto Etén before leaving Lima, but he'd been told he'd have no problem doing so on his arrival: dozens, even hundreds of them, took people back and forth between the two towns each day. He had managed to reserve a hotel in downtown Chiclayo, close to the square. It didn't offer full board, but the price was right, and as he was only staying one night, he could dispense with luxuries.

He'd spent his days before leaving Lima trying to follow the footsteps of Lalo Molfino, but he hadn't managed to find out much. The boy with the patent leather shoes seemed to have come and gone in the capital without leaving a trace. At the Hospital Obrero, Toño had been met by a wall of silence. He'd wanted to know how Lalo had ended up there, being uninsured and probably penniless, and which doctors had tended to him, but all anyone would tell him was what he'd already learned from Cecilia Barraza, that no one had claimed the body and he'd been buried in a common grave. It wasn't even clear why Lalo had left Chiclayo for Lima. There were gaps between his tenures in Durand Flores's Perú Negro and Cecilia Barraza's touring company; to keep from starving, he would have needed to find work in one of the music halls or bars, but so far, Toño had found no leads.

His research struggles caused the irritation in his arms and legs to return. All he had to do was close his eyes and he could see a rat leaping toward his face. He didn't understand why it was so hard to pick up Lalo's trail, and the more he thought about it, the more unfair it seemed—everything, but especially that unknown genius's fate. One afternoon, when leaving the National Library in downtown Lima, frustrated that he'd wasted another endless day without making any progress, the inevitable happened, the thing he'd managed to avoid for so long. He took a bus deeper into the city, then walked to the place where he would catch a minibus for Villa El Salvador, and all at once, he felt certain that an alley rat had climbed into his shirt. He stopped in the middle of the street, unconcerned about the passersby, unbuttoned his jacket, tore off his shirt, and held the pocket mirror he always carried with him so he could see his back. No animal was in sight. He was naked from the waist up, to the astonishment of those around him. As he quickly dressed again, he told himself how stupid this had been. But the fear was irresistible, the panic descended on him like rain, he shivered with desperation, *I've got to find a bathroom*, he thought, somewhere that he could strip off his pants, maybe his shirt, maybe his shoes—imagine if the rodents had slipped under his socks and were gnawing at his feet, or worse, if they'd crawled into his underwear. This had never happened, of course—only once had a rat actually fallen on him, that time in Malambo. But the terror of one of those creatures sneaking into his clothing, tail thrashing, drove him mad, and he would check himself over with the mirror for seconds that felt like hours. His panic made a fool of him, whenever and wherever it struck, but there was nothing he could do about it. He never told Matilde of these incidents, to keep from ruining her golden years, he told himself.

Despite how little information he had, Toño Azpilcueta had assembled voluminous notes for his book-to-be, and had even come up with a provisional title: *A Nip of Champagne, Brother?* That was an homage to his friend and patron, Collau. One day, when they were talking about Toño's book, which was then little more than an inspiration, they heard people taking to the streets to celebrate the news that the terrorist Abimael Guzmán had been captured. Toño ran out to take part in the jubilation; Collau took a bottle from the fridge before joining him. "A nip of champagne, brother?" he asked, and that jubilant tone stuck with Toño, who wanted his book to be festive, centered on the two fundamental themes of brotherhood and *huachafería*.

It was absurd, he had emphasized in one of his notes, to consider this word, as many dictionaries did—up to and including dictionaries of the regionalisms of Peru—as a synonym of "flamboyance" or "affectation." No, there was more than affectation in the country's *huachafería*: there was a distinct way of understanding the world, innocent, tender, less refined than intuitive, common to all classes of society. He would use Lalo Molfino's patent leather shoes as its symbol. There was the humble *huachafería* of the Peruvian Indians, the mestizo *huachafería* characteristic of the middle classes, and even the rich showed their own sort of *huachafería* when they tried to pass themselves off as noblemen or the descendants of noblemen, challenging each other to duels according to the code of the Marqués de Cabriñana, as if they might thereby turn lily-white, shedding any last trace of indigenous blood.

Because the true Peruvian was mestizo, *cholo* as they said: on that point, the indigenists had been emphatic, in particular the great Cuzco author José Uriel García in his 1930 book *The New Indian*. But Uriel García's conclusions were vague, and it was Toño's task to expand on his insights and grasp the mysteries of Peru's *huachafería* and the mingling of cultures as expressed in creole music, in the vals, the pasillo, the marinera, the polka, the *huainito serrano*, which were played on the guitar, but just as well on the cajon, the jawbone, the piano, the cornet, the rattle, the harp, the lute, the harmonica, and endless numbers of instruments from the mountains, the forest, and the coast that had enriched and enlivened the country's popular culture. There were vain intellectuals—he exempted Dr. José Durand Flores, of course—who looked down on these expressions of the nation's artistic spirit because they didn't sufficiently resemble French or English models. They didn't understand *huachafería*, which was beautiful and true only because it arose from uncorrupted feeling, from the intuitive wisdom of a world that preceded the artificiality and posturing endemic among those writers who only read in French and English, and were indifferent to, if not contemptuous of, the magazines where Toño published.

In his book, which no one would be able to put down, Lalo Molfino would emerge as the undisputed master of *huachafería*, a man who had passed through life like a breath of air and without knowing it, without meaning to, had created with his guitar what had transported Toño to moments of bliss of unequaled intensity. When Toño saw him in Abajo el Puente, he'd understood for the first time why he had devoted his life to the nation's folk culture: a folk culture that had reached its maturity at the end of the nineteenth century, with Felipe Pinglo Alva, the bohemian composers of the Old Guard, the *faites* of the Palizada, and their hundred rivals, but that had been gestating for three hundred years, as the violence of the discovery of America and the Spanish conquests gave way to the future Peru, that brutal interweaving of Spanish and Indian from which the Peruvian people were born.

Some say the origins of the Peruvian vals are to be found in the fandango of Seville; others, like the historian Manuel Zanutelli Rosas, claim it migrated from Austria with the music of Johann Strauss. No one would ever agree, but what did it matter where it came from? What counted was that it existed, now and forever. The music was a myth, its founding father, Pinglo Alva, was a myth, and all myths are born of confusion and contradictions.

On his way to Chiclayo, Toño smiled, feeling happy. His book, he told himself, would be ideological and would defend a thesis. Would he be able to publish it? Of course. Of course he would find people who were interested in his theories and willing to underwrite the printing costs. It might be a simple volume, with cheap paper, the letters laid out by hand by those relics, the brilliant and pompous old typesetters who still existed in some printing houses in Lima. *Huachafería*, that's what his book would be, all the better, Toño thought—and he wouldn't have the least compunction about admitting it. He himself was an eminent exemplar of *huachafería*. This idea made him laugh aloud, and some of his fellow passengers turned to look at him, disconcerted, asking themselves if he might be insane. Toño coughed, trying to cover for himself, as he looked out the window of the bus.

The sea was visible no more, as the highway had edged toward the mountains, but the sand, now gray, remained there amid the scant brush, crowned by white clouds, interrupted now and then by squalid little towns, minuscule, nameless—at least for him—where the bus would stop, letting passengers off and on. Happily, the vehicle was never filled.

The heat kept rising. The desert around him was mysterious. Those who knew said it was full of animals, and hunters would sneak in on the weekends to prey on them. There were rabbits in those dunes, lizards, spiders, even the occasional small fox. And of course, rats and mice of all shapes and sizes—the thought of them brought on a fit of disgust. He'd been sitting in the bus for hours, and his bones and buttocks had begun to ache.

He wondered if he would eat the local specialty in Chiclayo that night: rice with roast duck. Perhaps, with a glass of beer. But after more than eleven hours in that rattletrap, all he wanted was to sleep in a clean, comfortable bed.

When the journey ended, Toño asked for directions to his hotel, the Santa Rosa on the Avenida San José, and instead of taking a taxi, he went on foot, dragging with him his luggage and his suitcase full of index cards and notebooks. He was sore, but he was happy, and optimistic about what he would find. He stood at the beginning of a great adventure, but already he could see his book before him.

The city was pleasing to him, with its whitewashed houses, its stores with people rushing in and out. The Hotel Santa Rosa was more modest than he'd expected. His room had a fully equipped bathroom but no fan, and even after he threw the windows open, the heat was like a furnace. Tired, he stripped naked, not bothering to put on his pajamas, and lay down on the bed wondering if he could fall asleep in that inferno. Immediately, the mosquitos attacked him, and his mind turned to the nooks and crannies in the room where horrible rodents might lie in wait.

Nonetheless, he fell asleep quickly. He woke early the next day, before the clock had even struck six. He showered with warm water, shaved, and carefully combed his hair, putting on the same pants and underwear as the day before, but a clean shirt and socks. He was grateful that he'd had no nightmares, and he asked the yawning receptionist, a young man with the biblical name of Caifás, where to get breakfast. Half a block away, the young man replied, on the town square, there were many cafés already open, and he could catch a ride to Puerto Etén there for one *sol* fifty.

Under the tall trees—tamarinds, he thought—he found a table on the reddish stone sidewalk. The city's life was already bubbling with intensity: people passed by noisily or formed groups waiting for someone or something on the square, maybe some work. There was a huge cinema there, probably closed, the city hall, and the cathedral, which required a suit jacket and hat for entry. He ordered a breakfast of fried eggs, tamales, buttered bread, and café con leche.

While he waited to be served, he looked at his pocket journal and checked the pencils in his jacket, making sure they were well sharpened. He bought *La Industria*, a local newspaper, and found in it the same international news he'd read in Lima the day before.

His waiter told him there were minibuses parked near the taxi stand to take passengers north and south. One of them could get him to Puerto Etén in half an hour, give or take. It wasn't far at all, but the road was unpaved. Toño ate his breakfast calmly, savoring every bite. It was still cool out, and since Puerto Etén was by the sea, he wouldn't roast there the way he had the night before. He remembered now that some time back, a Peruvian poet had published a book called *Puerto Etén*. What was his name again? He'd need to read it, in case there was any mention of Lalo Molfino. Rice with roast duck—he'd eat that on his way back. They probably had it in all the surrounding restaurants.

VIII

As I've said, one of the most picturesque characters in La Palizada was Toni Lagarde from Miraflores, who was typical of the sort of young white people who in those days fancied themselves troublemakers. We're still close friends, and he's still alive and kicking, and I hope he will be for many more years. I heard his story from his own lips: a story which is far from common in this Lima of ours, overrun with racial prejudice (not to mention, thanks to the Shining Path, bullets, blackouts, and dogs hanged from posts).

Toni had entered the University of La Molina to study agronomy, and had fallen in with the group of toughs led by Karamanduka, and on their nights of adventure, they fooled around on the guitar, sang, and danced the valses and marineras of the backstreets of Lima, getting into trouble whenever trouble crossed their paths.

Toni was one of the youngest of the group, and he always kept his hair neat, with a buttoned-up sports coat, snug pants, red socks, shined shoes, and a white handkerchief that he took out whenever a marinera played. (I've seen photos of him as a boy, and he looked quite the dandy.) He had let his hair grow out, and it fell in blond locks to his shoulders. He was ivory-white with big blue eyes that narrowed when he sang or danced.

Toni Lagarde always wanted to return to a street in Mirones where motley parties were thrown and where the ever-unruly La Palizada was welcome. And the members of La Palizada wondered why. What they discovered was that he was in pursuit of Lala Solórzano, a thin, shapely woman, black, saucy, and brash, who gracefully danced the vals, the marinera, and the *huainito*, and had sparks in her sprightly eyes. She was a seasoned flirt, the way the women from Lima are, though she was no older than sixteen or seventeen. Karamanduka and his friends ribbed Toni endlessly about his fascination with her.

One fine day, Toni Lagarde admitted it—he was in love with Lala—and he warned everyone to stay away from her: she was his, his; he didn't want to hear any compliments spoken to her, any invitations to dance. Whoever dared would have to deal with him, and he wasn't one for jokes. He was tipsy when he said this, and no one paid him any mind. But soon they saw the couple holding hands, dancing every night—she seemed resigned never to dance with anybody else—always together, batting their eyes at each other, kissing like a couple in love.

The men of La Palizada asked him one day: Was this affair of his in Mirones something serious? Did he not realize he was a rich kid from Miraflores and she was a black girl from Lima's most hardscrabble neighborhood? Surely he just wanted to bed her—or was there more to it? Toni turned bright red, tried not to answer, then sternly confessed that there was *something more* with Lala Solórzano, that he *loved* her, that what they had was real. The whole gang chided him—"Come on, Toni, don't tell us you've got a taste for the dark meat like that, what, are you going to marry her? We don't believe you, and your parents sure as hell won't, if you've actually got the balls to tell them."

Toni, though, wasn't one to be pushed around. He did tell his parents, they shrieked like the damned, and his father threatened to throw him out of the house. In a fit of pride, Toni packed his bags, left his parents' home, checked into a rooming house, and never returned. He quit his agronomy studies and took a job in the Lima city government, where he remained until his retirement. Naturally, Lala's parents wound up scorning her, too, because she had shacked up with Toni instead of marrying in the church; that was un-christian, living in sin. Toni was eighteen at the time, and Lala's parents warned them to stay away until they'd married, and they treated their daughter as a stranger until the wedding three years later.

Everyone in La Palizada took for granted that this infatuation between the fancy boy and the dark-skinned girl from Mirones wouldn't last. He was from a good family, while Lala was half-illiterate. Her father was a part-time bricklayer for a company that built houses for the rich and her mother was a washerwoman and occasional seamstress. Her father had a knack for the cajon as well, and sometimes gave lessons on their street.

The two young people didn't care what others said; they loved each other, and their love abided. They surprised everyone again when it turned out Lala was pregnant, and instead of going to an abortionist and getting rid of the kid, the way so many did in Lima at the time, Toni and Lala announced they were keeping it. They still went to parties in Mirones, holding hands, just as blissful as they'd been on the day they first met.

Lala's belly and their happiness grew in unison. When the time came, she was placed in a maternity ward in downtown Lima, where she gave birth to a little girl. It must have been funny, seeing them walk the streets of Lima, him with snow-white skin and blond hair, her dark and sultry, and their little girl with the same tight curls as her mother, dozing away in her carriage. But Toni Lagarde never regretted his infatuation, and their marriage endured, despite everything, all the way through to his retirement.

It was around then that I met them, and both already had gray hair. I was working on a report for some newspaper or other, and I went to interview them, and we soon became friends. We have lunch together sometimes, and Lala makes a quince jam that's simply to die for. They used to have a place in Surquillo—that's where I visited them most often—but you could still find them strolling in downtown Lima or through the parks in Miraflores, or on their way to the backstreet where her parents lived. After their marriage, with the blessing of the church (and with La Palizada brilliant in their supporting role), they were welcome again in the hovel in Mirones with their daughter, little Carmencita Carlota, in tow.

Toni's parents were stern, though, and held on to their bitterness till the end, never opening the doors of their home to him again. Only his mother deigned to see him on occasional Sundays at the church in Miraflores, before Mass at noon. Toni was a changed man, sober and serious, and though he'd come out to greet the members of La Palizada, it was rare that he'd dance. Nor would Lala. They were happy in their way, to the surprise of all. They had their disagreements, the way all couples do, but despite expectations, they remained close. They aged well, and were a handsome couple who never lost their flirtatious air.

Theirs was the only lasting relationship to come of La Palizada. The rest of the revelers and bohemians died young, or remained single as their station in life gradually worsened. The few who made it to old age did so poor. Some even became beggars.

Not Karamanduka, of course. He grew wealthy and famous in Lima, with his theatrical adaptations and his excellent valses and marineras. The magazine *Variedades* photographed him in formal wear at the height of his glory. If there was one thing he always had, it was a good ear for creole music.

Toni and Lala live in Breña now, close to Colegio La Salle, where I studied, and whenever I visit them, they offer me a tea or hot coffee and toasted buns with those quince preserves of Lala's that I swear get better every time I try them. It's a pleasure, hearing them talk of the old days and the trouble La Palizada used to get into. Carmencita Carlota is older now. She's had boyfriends, but has never married, and works at a company that provides catering services to factories. She's a loving daughter, and a fine-looking one, as mixed-race women often are, with a swimmer's body and eyes that could stop you in your tracks and mesmerize you. A kind woman, she always asks why I don't visit more often. She likes me coming because her parents never tell her the stories I always manage to shake out of them. There's nothing I like more than hearing their memories of the days when that music overtook the nation, becoming something truly Peruvian.

And now, to emphasize the importance of the subject at

hand, to bring my story into the present and reveal the urgency of it, here's a bit of politics and current events, a taste of the blackouts and gunshots that plague Villa El Salvador. One day, I came home a little late and found Matilde and my daughters frightened because there was a woman hiding in one of our bedrooms. She was crying, and she said there were two guerrillas outside from the Shining Path who wanted to kill her. I had seen them at the door. They had greeted me politely. They didn't look like thugs or gunslingers, but she swore otherwise. I went back outside, and they were gone, vanished into the night. We offered the woman a coffee and, jittery, she accepted. Her name was María Elena Moyano. She lived in Pachacámac, one of the neighborhoods in Villa El Salvador, and the Shining Path, who were trying to take over there, wanted to kill her because she opposed them and had denounced them vehemently in public.

Of course, they did end up murdering her, and not long afterward. So things go in our country. Let's shed a few tears for that brave woman, and invoke the grace and good cheer of Peruvian music in the hope that the hatreds that divide brother from brother will soon dissolve.

IX

Just as they'd told him, he'd reached Puerto Etén in half an hour. The enchantment of the place lay in the docks, in the sea, in the crescent of sandy beach beside the esplanade from the fifties, in the stillness of the abandoned railroad station. The neighboring town, Ciudad Etén, was full of factories and shops and signs of prosperity. Endless children swam in the sea, shouted, ran, chased each other. All the homes were of wood—old fishermen's houses, they must have been—and now they were neatly restored, with their little covered porches, a lot of them serving as hotels.

Toño strolled through the city and later to a square called the Plaza Juan Mejía Baca, named for a publisher and bookseller whose shop was just steps from the University of San Marcos on Jirón Azángaro in Lima. The heat was awful, of course, as were the clouds of mosquitos. Toño hadn't cared for the thought of dragging his luggage through the city, so he'd taken a room at the first place he found, El Rincón del Norte, which stood right there on the square. His room was small, with a bed and a nightstand and windows facing the sea. There appeared to be no nooks or crannies where rats might lurk. Puerto Etén's downtown, with its two plazas, was a pleasant sight. On his first night out, he'd seen the offices of a political party, Acción Popular, with a photo on the door of Belaúnde Terry, who had served twice as president of the republic. There was a church nearby, but it was closed, and since he was dripping sweat, his forehead and hands smoldering, he stopped somewhere to have a beer.

He'd imagined his work would be easy, but two days later, he still hadn't met a single person who'd even heard of Lalo Molfino. Toño had thought he'd be the pride of the town, a local hero, that even the cobblestones there would weep at the mention of his harmonious guitar. But no. He'd asked in the pharmacies, at the cafés, in the factories, among the people in the shops in Ciudad Etén; he'd asked workers and passersby, and no one knew a thing about the most important person ever born there. How was it possible? In despair, Toño had turned to the police, who were stationed in a half-built structure where he'd found a kindly officer who shrugged before asking if Toño might be referring to that Mexican-sounding music everyone in the north of Peru was on about.

"Lalo Molfino, you said? No, I've never heard of him. I think there was an Italian priest with that same last name. An Italian, that's right, or a European anyway, I'm pretty sure. But he was already dead by the time I came here from Tumbes, which is where I'm from. I said dead, or maybe it was just that he wasn't in Puerto Etén anymore. Now that I think about it, it seems like he went back to Italy. People around here loved him. They even gave him a special certificate when he left."

Toño returned to his hotel, where he had a drink on the terrace as he looked out at the foamy sea and the crescent of beach, now abandoned by the boys and girls who had spent the day splashing in its russet waters. Exhausted, he told himself he'd made a mistake. He was at the edge of despair, ready to throw in the towel, when the innkeeper told him someone was looking for him. A man appeared, a former member of the Civil Guard who introduced himself with a formal bearing. "My name's Pedro Caballero," he said, and explained that he'd been told at the police station that there was a man from Lima walking around asking questions about Lalo Molfino.

Caballero had a baby face, but with the slightest wisp of beard. It was hard to say what age he might be. He limped, helping himself along with a cane. He wore a military man's boots and cap with a visor, but otherwise he was dressed in civvies. He told Toño that, because of a lack of officers, the Civil Guard had allowed him to stay on in some form or other despite his bum leg, which he'd broken playing soccer and now had wrapped in bandages.

Lalo, he said, had been his best friend since he was a kid. They'd been classmates at a little school opened in Puerto Etén by a remarkable Italian priest named Father Molfino.

Toño asked the man if he'd like a cold beer. At last, he'd found someone who could tell him something, and this meant Lalo wasn't a ghost, as he had been beginning to fear. Pedro Caballero told him Lalo had lived in Puerto Etén. When they were young, he and Pedro had been inseparable. Then Lalo had gotten a wild hair—that was typical of him—and took off for Piura or Chiclayo to make his way in a creole group called the Troubadours of the North or something like that. He hadn't even left a note letting Pedro know. That was Lalo, though, and you had to take him as he was. He was an artist, and artists were impulsive and hard to deal with, every last one of them.

Toño asked him to wait while he ran to his room for his notebook. He didn't want to miss anything that might prove important. He came back sweating, thirsty for another beer despite his finances, but thinking that Collau had lent him money to research, not to wet his whistle. He bombarded Pedro with questions, starting from the beginning, with Lalo's origins. Toño supposed that someone close to Lalo, his mother or his father, perhaps, had taught him the guitar, but Pedro Caballero told him otherwise: Lalo Molfino had been an orphan. He never knew who his real parents were.

"And where he came from?" Toño asked, scribbling frantically.

"He never knew that either, I think," Pedro said with a shrug. "Neither did Father Molfino, who raised him. At least he said he didn't."

"I'll never forget it," Father Molfino said, his lips vibrating against his half-toothless mouth. "Brrr. It was freezing that night in Puerto Etén, young man!" ("Young man" was the term he always used when addressing Pedro Caballero.)

On that chilly night, Father Molfino had been lying down with the lights dimmed in the fisherman's cabin that now served as a rectory when he heard a knock at the door. A child's voice called his name: "Father Molfino, Father Molfino." The priest was groggy, but he got up, threw a blanket over his shoulders, and opened up. The boy knocking had fear in his eyes and in his voice, and he looked exhausted. Father Molfino knew him well. He'd attended Mass as an altar boy on many a Sunday.

"Miss Domitila's dying, Father, and she wants you to give her the sacrament."

"Can't she wait till tomorrow to die?" Father Molfino

asked, not entirely joking. He and the boy were shivering. The temperature dropped dramatically at night in Puerto Etén.

"She can't," the boy said. "She's sick, I think she's near the end. She might even be gone before we get there."

"And where does Domitila live?" Father Molfino asked as he bundled up.

"She lived far away," Pedro Caballero told Toño, pointing past him vaguely. "Over there. Past one of the dumps, the oldest one, because there's several of them. At least three that I know of. The biggest one, Reque, is just outside of town. You can imagine: miles and miles of trash, and flies and rats all over."

Father Molfino donned his cassock and filled his basket with all he would need to perform extreme unction on poor Miss Domitila. He knew her; he'd served as her confessor several times in recent weeks, he knew she was coughing and vomiting, but he didn't know it had gone so far. He lifted the young man onto his motorcycle, and together they rode along the shore. In the sky was a round moon and a sea of stars. The child guided the priest down a road that led out of the city, and ten minutes later, he told him to stop. The smell was repugnant, and the priest was shocked to see the boy walking toward a waste heap.

"Domitila lives there?" he asked.

"Further on," the boy said. "It's not too far, Father."

"It's full of roaches and rats that way," Father Molfino protested.

"You think I don't know?" the boy responded. "I already got bit when I was leaving to find you."

Father Molfino explained that he'd had to walk deep

into the trash pits, around a corner, to a miserable hut on a hill. "There's a whole neighborhood there, of people poorer than you can imagine. Domitila had died already, I'm pretty sure. She lived alone. The kid was a neighbor. They weren't related, but he took care of her, ran errands for her and so on."

"Wait," Toño Azpilcueta said. "She actually lived out there past the trash pits?"

"I had no choice but to walk through there," Father Molfino said. "That's where Domitila lived. That's where she got her meals from, the poor thing. She used to say people always threw out something you could eat there. Leftovers, scraps, you had to get to them quick, though, before the rats and roaches did, the flies and the mosquitos. There were thousands of insects there, and bats, too, Domitila used to say. Then I heard this sound, like . . ."

"Like what, Father?" Pedro Caballero asked, his leg not yet crippled, proud in his Civil Guard uniform, with his revolver at his side.

"Just like what it was. You know: the cry of a little boy," Father Molfino responded, eyes wide and gesturing with bony hands. "I was done there, I'd given the last rites and Domitila was gone, and that kid, I forget his name, he was going to stay there beside her and pray for her eternal soul. I was walking back through the rubbish, ready to go home. I kept flapping my hands around, trying to scare off the mosquitos and flies, and I stepped hard, hoping to startle the roaches and rats. That damned dump. Imagine it, a whole field of trash, smelling of everything noxious you could imagine, and the only way I could get back to Puerto Etén was to cross through it. So as I said, I heard it. Very, very soft. Could it really be what I thought it was? Well, yes. It was the cry of a young boy. It had to be; I was certain of it."

"Father Molfino spoke excellent Spanish," Pedro Caballero said. "But as soon as you heard him, you knew he was Italian. He didn't speak his words so much as sing them. Oh, and I should have said, cheers, buddy!"

Toño Azpilcueta knocked his beer glass against Caballero's: "Cheers!"

"So his mother just abandoned him out in the middle of the dump, to be eaten by rats? Are you serious?" Pedro Caballero asked Father Molfino, with a creeping sense of dread.

"I know, I still have dreams about it, I have for a long time," Father Molfino said. "Twenty-two years it's been, and I've never told a soul what happened. You're the first one, well, apart from the justice of the peace who gave me guardianship over the kid. I told him the story, and he asked me the same question I'd asked myself: How is it the rats didn't get to him? I guess it was his crying, it scared them off. Rats have very delicate ears. The boy wasn't wailing, it was more of a soft whine, I could hear it, though—I had good hearing then, not like now, it's started to give out with the years, same as my eyes. *What was that?* I asked myself. And I knew it was a child crying. Well, how could I just keep walking, knowing someone had left a newborn there in the midst of all that filth? Can you imagine? So I gathered my courage and dug around there in the dark, I kicked at the rats and cockroaches, and tried to find out where those helpless moans were coming from."

"I guess his mother didn't have it in her to do away with

him," Pedro Caballero murmured. "Still, she abandoned him there. Did you ever find out who she was?"

"I didn't," Father Molfino said, shaking his head. "A poor woman, desperate, there's no doubt about that. There's lots of them around here, people who have nothing and are capable of anything. Hunger, it eats away at your conscience. Imagine the poor woman. What it takes to leave your newborn there for the rats to sink their teeth into."

"So you found him," Pedro said.

"Eventually," Father Molfino replied. Again, his voice trembled as he remembered. "It took a long time, you know. I can't say how long I spent out there, really, half-terrified of what kind of awful creatures there must have been marauding in the muck. And then I saw him. He was wrapped up in a blanket. I picked him up and he kept crying. He wanted to nurse, of course. He wanted his mother's breast. He was a skeleton, the poor kid. I still recall quite clearly the way I could feel every one of his bones beneath my fingers. Walking out of there with that boy in my arms, the tears sprang to my eyes. I thought I'd forgotten how to cry, but no. That day I learned I still could."

"Did Lalo know?" Toño asked, putting his pencil down for a moment, and feeling closer to his subject, somehow, knowing about the rats that had been closing in on him. He wondered how often he would dream of them in the days to come. "Did he know his mother had abandoned him at a dump on the outskirts of town, when he was still just a baby?"

"I never told him," Father Molfino said.

"I don't know," Pedro Caballero responded. "I spoke to

the priest about all this after Lalo was grown. He'd had a fit, the way he often did, and had run off from one day to the next, to Chiclayo or Piura, as I think I told you before, and he didn't even say goodbye to the man who had saved him, who had adopted him, who had placed him in the school here. Santa Margarita, the school was called. I went there, too. Father Molfino named it that on account of some virgin saint from over in Italy that he used to pray to. Could Lalo have found out where he'd come from? Maybe, I don't know. There were rumors around the school, but nobody ever said anything to him that I know of."

"Is Father Molfino still around?" Toño asked, taking a sip of his now-lukewarm beer.

"No, sir. He got the feeling his time was short and he left for Italy," Pedro Caballero said. "There was a big farewell for him in Puerto Etén, and even the mayor pinned a medal to his chest. I don't know what ever happened to old Father Molfino. He has to have died, I'd say."

"How long ago was all this?" Toño Azpilcueta asked. He had a sour taste in his mouth and thought he could see rats and roaches all around.

"Oh, a hell of a lot of years," Pedro Caballero said. "A hell of a lot. And I guess I'm the only one around here who even knows that whole story about the dump and everything."

The two men had lost their appetites with all the talk of trash and vermin, and they refused the potato and beef croquettes the waiter at El Rincón del Norte offered them. A few more beers, though—that was what they needed to put those repellent images behind them.

"To give you some idea," Pedro said, "Father Molfino was already here when I was born. My mother said he was the one who baptized me. He legally adopted Lalo, and that's why they shared a last name. He was a good man, the priest. When he founded Santa Margarita, he ran it like a public school, though it wasn't one, strictly speaking, and the students didn't pay a cent, or at least most of them didn't. A lot of boys and girls from Puerto Etén studied there. He was a pioneer in that way, mixing boys and girls, you know. Most of us who went there ended up at the Colegio Nacional for secondary school, but not Lalo—he'd discovered the guitar. And from that moment on, the instrument was his life."

Toño nodded, savoring the second beer the waiter had set down on the table. It was cold, but he knew it would warm up quickly.

"I don't know where he found the thing, but this being Puerto Etén, it was probably in the trash. It was old, beat up, with no strings, if you can believe that. No strings! But he took it and he brought it back to life. And then, well, that guitar was everything to him. I know you must think I'm exaggerating, but I'm not. He put strings on it, replaced the pegs, painted it. Not painted, oiled it, I mean. From then on, every time you saw him, he had that guitar with him. And far as I know, he learned to play it on his own, too. I never heard of anyone teaching him. That's why he quit school, to spend day and night practicing guitar. It drove Father Molfino out of his mind. He wanted the boy to finish high school at the Colegio Nacional, but Lalo couldn't have cared less. That guitar was his life, as I said. And boy, could he play."

"That he could," Toño agreed. "I'll never forget the first time I heard him. That's what brought me here. But let's stick to the subject. What was Lalo's relationship with the priest like?"

"Strange," Pedro Caballero said. "Everything about it was strange, like a lot of things in Lalo's life. He never treated the priest like a father, he always treated him like a churchman. He respected him, but I'm not certain he ever loved him."

"And the other kids at school?" Toño asked. "Did he have friends? Girlfriends?"

"Lord, no," Pedro Caballero said. "He didn't get along well with the rest. He was cagey, suspicious. And people said, you know, that's weird, living with a priest. People didn't get it. But no one threw it in his face, because Lalo, he'd headbutt you right in the nose. He was a fighter—a little guy, but he wouldn't put up with nonsense. He wasn't easy to be friends with. I was furious when I found out he'd gone to Chiclayo or Piura or whatever without saying goodbye. It must have cut Father Molfino deep. But like I told you, Lalo, he was a strange bird."

"He had to have had a teacher, though," Toño Azpilcueta objected. "You can't just learn the guitar on your own. Especially not how he played."

"Who was going to give him lessons around here?" Pedro nearly shouted. "Here, in Puerto Etén. Have you seen any guitar teachers? Because I haven't, and like I told you, Lalo was one of the least sociable people you could imagine, he'd never have sat patiently at another man's feet. He talked to me, but beyond that, I don't remember him ever getting along with anybody."

"So he left the village school and that was it for his education?" Toño asked.

"As far as I know," Pedro responded. "I didn't see him much after that, on account of that damned guitar. Anyway, what would be the point of him studying when that was the only thing that interested him? Tell me something, though. You must know a lot about these things—what kind of player was Lalo?"

"The best I've heard in my life," Toño said. "And you're right, I do know about these things. You can take my word for it, I've heard hundreds of guitarists, Peruvians and foreigners as well. And no one could touch him."

"Now, I heard him many a time, but I'd never have guessed that," Pedro confessed. "So Lalo, he was really something, then?"

"He was a genius. More than a genius. He was divine, sublime, you name it."

"I must say, you've given me something to think about," Pedro Caballero said, scratching his head. "And you're writing a book about him, huh? I hope you find a place for me in those pages. After all, I'm the one who gave you all this information about Lalo, isn't that right?"

Toño Azpilcueta stayed five days in Puerto Etén—three more than he'd planned on. He spent that additional time morning, noon, and night with the very accommodating Pedro Caballero, drinking beers at El Rincón del Norte along with dozens of the latter's friends who had known Lalo Molfino at Santa Margarita. Most of them could hardly remember him; a few couldn't at all, and made things up just to put on a show for this Liman who'd gotten the idea of writing a book about some mestizo from their town that he'd decided was a genius.

His most important find in those three extra days of

searching came from a lawyer named Juan Quiroga, a man who had neither known Lalo Molfino nor attended school with him but who brought Toño the statement Father Molfino had made to the police upon finding the boy in a trash heap, in which he declared his intention of adopting Lalo if no one else claimed him. It was an invaluable document, and the lawyer was kind enough to give him a photocopy of it, which Toño tucked very carefully into his briefcase.

Toño spent an entire night thinking about the first clumsy chords Lalo must have drawn from that resuscitated guitar, and what they must have sounded like in the night in Puerto Etén. Tears came to his eyes in the solitude of his rented room, where he could hear the waves crashing as the wind blew over the rugged sea. At fifty, he was turning sentimental. But why? What made him weep at the mere memory of that kid from Puerto Etén who had played like a dream? They'd both been raised by men from Italy, even if Toño's father had a Basque last name. They'd both felt some kind of breach between themselves and Peru that they'd managed to repair by devoting themselves to creole music, the most Peruvian of all the arts. The vals had sufficed to fill any emptiness, any lack. As he learned more about Lalo Molfino, Toño started to imagine that he, too, had been picked up off the street, perhaps from some trash heap, in mortal panic, to be raised by a man from elsewhere. His rootlessness, his uncertainty about his origins, was a torment to him. Human beings weren't atoms, he told himself, they weren't made to navigate through life on their own; human beings were made to form part of something bigger, a community, a fatherland capable of protecting them and giving them meaning. What was a man without that tribe? Little more than a child dropped in a dump, left to the mercy of rats. Toño dried his eyes with his fingers and pulled the sheet over himself despite the heat. He was afraid a mouse, maybe a tiny one, might creep up through a crack in the floorboards. There was only one idea that calmed him, that he held on to tight until he fell asleep: that he had found something to devote his life to—his book on Lalo Molfino. He had important things to say.

X

The Peruvian vals is a social institution: it was not created, like other music, to be played or heard in solitude. Not in the least. The vals requires a group of three, four, or more to be played or, better said, brought to life. And this is why, from its beginnings in the late nineteenth and early twentieth centuries, it was always closely associated with groups: the famous Los Morochucos, of course, featuring Óscar Avilés, Augusto Ego-Aguirre, and Alejandro Cortez; the legendary duo Montes and Manrique, and the Abancay Trio, with César Santa Cruz, José Moreno, and Pablo Casas. César Santa Cruz Gamarra states that José Moreno was close friends with Felipe Pinglo Alva and accompanied him selflessly "to the very end."

These groups always consisted of a singer and several musicians—guitarists, mostly, though other accompanying instruments appeared as the music made its mark on different parts of society. For the upper classes, there were pianos and violins, and for the humbler people, lutes, cajones, castanets, cornets, harmonicas, even cog rattles in more recent years. We must sing the praises of Eduardo Montes and César Augusto Manrique, who, at the beginning of the twentieth century, when no one was pressing records in Peru, arrived in New York with 182 Peruvian compositions, from which ninety-one records were made. According to the authors I draw on, José Antonio Lloréns Amico and Rodrigo Chocano Paredes, this demonstrates that already in 1911, "there was a considerable volume of widely popular creole music" in Peru.

Around 1930, the first songbooks and music centers appeared. The latter were institutions devoted to the memory of the great artists and composers. The first of these was the Centro Musical Carlos A. Saco, followed by another dedicated to Felipe Pinglo Alva after his death. At these places, people could drink and celebrate the art of the country's musicians, and they helped popularize creole music. Jesús Vásquez and La Limeñita y Ascoy, a brother-and-sister duo, appeared frequently at the Centro Musical Carlos A. Saco, while the Centro Social Musical Felipe Pinglo Alva had many members but only one leading light: María Jesús Jiménez.

I've always felt profound admiration for these groups that were born with the vals. Not only mere musicians, they were friends who shared much more than love for creole music. From their enthusiasm for the nation's melodies, there arose an awareness of collectivity, the notion that they belonged to a single country they should be proud of. It's a shame that no one recalls the oldest of those pioneers, those voices, many of them women. In the earliest days, songs weren't written down, and if we know these artists' names at all, it is thanks largely to scholars who mention them in their memoirs, among them the Frenchman Gérard Borras, who wrote a splendid study of the Peruvian vals. A gathering of such people, where one could listen to their stories—that would offer a true history of Peru.

The vals took root in our country, spreading first among the down-and-out, then climbing to the middle class and the aristocracy, and it has retained its position, touching every Peruvian family without exception. I remember an article by Ruperto Castillo in *Folklore Nacional* in which he tells of his surprise upon visiting a lost village in the middle of the Amazon where, he had supposed, civilization had not yet arrived. While there, he heard a Peruvian vals sung by the indigenous people in their own language. With its arrival in the deepest heart of the jungle, who can deny that it is truly a national music?

When I say that the vals inspires conviviality, I mean this in all senses of the word. Who ever played a vals by himself? No one but Lalo Molfino. And his case was exceptional, so for that reason, let us forgive him. If you played as he did, you would naturally disdain the idea of sharing the stage. The bands that play the vals are and have always been a goad to friendship and solidarity, a remedy for individualism and selfishness, a font of entertainments that can only be had with others: dancing and revelry, inveterate pastimes in our country. The vals has given birth to hundreds, thousands of groups in the capital and in the provinces, promoting amity and that sense of fellowship the country is so known for, not to mention romances and who knows how many weddings.

I don't mean to say we're a jubilant land, like Brazil, for example, where people dance half-naked in the streets during their famous Carnival, but we are a friendly country, indeed a country where friendship is indispensable, a place of laughter, a place where people celebrate birthdays and weep together at funerals. And what is companionship if not that? A way of relating to others, of building bridges. And this is what the vals is, too: nostalgia for the past, affection, companionship, and, of course, love.

Because—I can't deny it—the vals is highly erotic as well. Let us return to that couple that joined the two extremes of Peruvian society: Toni Lagarde, from the crème de la crème of Miraflores, and Lala Solórzano, the impish black beauty from Mirones. What has kept them together so long? Eros, what else? Despite their years, their nights must still be full of joy, adventure, exploration, and happiness. I will hold my tongue at this point out of respect for any ladies who might be reading.

Eroticism is something we must treat with delicacy—I wouldn't want to offend any priests or old dames. But I am convinced that whoever listens to the Peruvian vals, and especially whoever dances to it, will sooner or later fall prey to passion, which will grow and reach a boiling point.

When couples meet to dance, they get aroused, and they start to lust for each other. Maybe they wind up in bed, maybe they don't. Either way, the vals has done its job. After that, it's up to the couple themselves to perform the work of love (*and lovemaking*, I was going to add, but I shall silence myself in case the priests are reading), as Toni Lagarde and Lala Solórzano did with such success. There were numerous conflicts between the vals and the church in the nineteenth century. The bishops condemned it as immoral and indecent. Apparently, they took offense at the man's fingers grazing the woman's back—in those days, people danced at a distance—and they nearly forbade it. I've studied this, and I swear it's true. But the Catholic Church is nothing if not astute, and seeing the vals's immense popularity in all parts of society, it recognized how ill-guided a prohibition on the dance would be.

Not all music can boast the same effects as the creole vals: not the *yaravíes*, not the sorrowful norteños, tender, melancholy songs for one voice. Mariano Melgar from Arequipa is iconic here, though we should mention there are others who tried to leaven the *yaraví* and give it a more communal note. Melgar was a hero, a romantic composer who died fighting for Peru's independence alongside General Pumacahua during the latter's uprising, and I enjoy listening to *yaravíes*, especially his, when I'm in a melancholy mood. The lighter, happier styles don't say much to me—I prefer the vals, which brightens life in all its moments and can be listened to at any time: in the morning, while you're still yawning; at midday, over lunch; in the evening, at night, and naturally, while working, because the vals is inspiring and pushes you to action.

This action, of course, can take a naughtier turn, in women as well as men. Who hasn't felt this when dancing, when our bodies touch, and the night goes on, and we share secrets and open up to one another? And this closeness gives way to temptation, hunger, the devilish thoughts that occur to two people when they feel attraction redoubled by the irresistible lyrics of the vals. I spoke of love and sociability before, but this cruder sort of attraction is what I really had in mind.

Does this happen with every type of music we dance to? Not at all. Who would attribute such powers to the Argentine zapateo or the samba? The first of these is a solo dance, and when there is a duo, each person dances alone, concentrating on steps dictated by the music, a music that isolates and pulls people apart rather than pushing them together and inflaming them. Zapateo is a dance to be contemplated; the vals is meant to be lived in the flesh.

This is why it's found such widespread acceptance in our country, why it's brought people together, why it's served to combat prejudice and racism. When we talk about the vals and its virtues, we shouldn't forget all this, which is an important part of its charm.

XI

Toño Azpilcueta awoke thinking of Lucha Reyes, the singer who most resembled Lalo Molfino, he thought, both in her tragic life and in her early death. He remembered a documentary about her in which the director explained that her hardworking character had helped her survive the four hindrances she'd faced: being a woman, being black, being a singer, and being homely.

She was born into an enormous family in 1936 in the slums of Rímac, where the poorest of the poor lived at the time, and she spent several years in a convent, with the thought of becoming a nun, one presumes, as this was one of the few ways for a poor black woman to survive. She endured the threat of hunger, and she endured many other challenges, too. To her good fortune, she met El Negro Ferrando, who took her to sing for his Radio América program that accompanied the horse races. Ferrando was the announcer, and equestrian sports were his passion, but he did a great deal for creole music, as Toño knew, discovering any number of musicians—including Cecilia Barraza herself. On his show, they had a place to sing or play the guitar, the guiro, or the cajon, and if they were lucky, they'd become famous. Lucha Reyes was one of the lucky ones.

Toño remembered Lucha Reyes in the wigs she used to

wear when she sang—blonde, red, and white—her capacious voice belting out those valses that were the very symbol of Peru's humility and poverty. There was *huachafería* there, too, of course, in her febrile, bloody tales, her exaggerated sentimentalism, her endless mawkishness, which added, somehow, a special accent to the Peruvian vals, a vigor and a strength unknown to it before then. She transformed that soft, effeminate, well-mannered music into something raucous and yet refined, as Toño had stressed in his many articles praising her.

If only Negro Ferrando had discovered Lalo Molfino. He would have known how to get people's eyes on him. Toño imagined Ferrando stripping the title of "first guitarist of Peru" from Óscar Avilés and giving it to Lalo, making recordings of him, taking him all over the country so Peruvians of all stripes could see him and recognize his glory. Lalo had deserved that fate, and since Negro Ferrando hadn't been able to see to it, perhaps it fell to Toño to grant Lalo fame after death with his book.

Toño's musings on Lucha Reyes were a way of distracting himself from his final task in Puerto Etén before returning to Lima. He didn't want to do it—it disgusted him, the mere thought of it gave him gooseflesh—but he knew that to write his book, he needed to travel to Reque, that sea of waste that stretches as far as the eye can see, the place where Father Molfino had found Lalo when he was a boy.

Before breakfast, he hailed a taxi and informed the driver that he needed to visit the dump for the sake of his writing. The driver understood, and opened the door to let him in. A half hour later, Toño had crossed the bridge and was standing before the expanse of debris, which was as endless as the flies that swarmed his face, arms, and hands no sooner than he had gotten out of the vehicle. Covering his nose when he could, he stepped out into the rubbish, watching the trucks deposit their loads of black bags after making their rounds in the neighboring towns.

Incredibly, in the midst of that refuse, there was a cabin built of cast-off paper, fabric, boards, and bits of iron, with an old man living inside. Toño approached, hoping to interview him, and saw him half-submerged in the waste, as if seeking treasure, before he surfaced while shaking his head to knock away some creature that had attached itself to him. The matter-of-fact way he did so only worsened Toño's revulsion. He scratched himself—he couldn't help it—and felt damp, disgusting claws crawling all over his body, inflaming his skin. With a stick, the old man drove away a vulture keen on stealing one of his prized possessions from the muck. Toño thought he might faint. He wondered what Lalo Molfino had felt there, abandoned, enveloped in the stench, surrounded by viscous insects crawling over his body, and he couldn't bear it anymore. Everything was too foul, and there had to be rats and mice everywhere. In a panic, chased by a halo of putrescence and flies, he fled to the cab, where he found the driver swatting at the mosquitos buzzing around his face. "Did you find what you came for?" the man joked. Toño, shivering from head to toe, asked him to get them out of there as quickly as possible.

In his room, he took a long bath and changed his pants and underwear. He was tempted to leave behind the clothing he'd worn to the dump. But lacking much else to wear, he stuffed it reluctantly back into his suitcase and double-checked his other bag to make sure all his papers were in there. He went to pay, dragging his luggage, and found a man at the entrance who had been waiting for him. Toño didn't recognize him at first. He was tall and slumped, and, like many of the locals, wore overalls with a T-shirt and tennis shoes.

"I'm glad I found you before you left," he said, shaking Toño's hand. "I'm Jacobo Machado. I met you yesterday, but there were so many of us, I doubt you remember."

"Oh, I remember you well," Toño said. "Of course. You're one of Pedro's friends."

"That's correct," Machado confirmed. "I came here because I have some information I think might be useful to you. I should have told you yesterday, but I had a few too many and it slipped my mind. I didn't know Lalo personally, but I remembered this morning something I heard about him one time. The man who took him to Chiclayo to play in a creole group, and to Lima, too, maybe, was named Abanto."

That surprised Toño. "Abanto? Luis Abanto Morales?" He was the favorite son of Cajabamba in the Cajamarca region, one of the most famous singers and guitarists Peru had ever produced. "Let me tell you something: I was just on my way to breakfast. How about you come along. My treat?"

"I can't tell you if his last name was Morales," Machado said, crinkling his wide nose. "Abanto, that's all I can say for sure. I met him in Chiclayo. I don't know if he ever set foot in Puerto Etén. We had a couple of beers together, on his dime."

The two men walked to a café next door to the inn, where they ordered coffee and buttered toast and talked a long while. Jacobo Machado mentioned he'd formerly been a truck driver and a porter, and had taken loads from Puerto Etén to Chiclayo and elsewhere in Peru in a big, shiny rig they called the Heckler.

He'd done that for two or three years, the pay had been pretty good. And one night in Chiclayo, this Abanto guy was buying him beers, and the subject of Puerto Etén came up. "The best guitarist in Peru is from there, a young man named Lalo Molfino," Abanto told Jacobo, and he boasted he'd hired him to play in a band. "I remember him, you know, because that name, Abanto, it has a weird ring to it," Machado added.

"It does," Toño said. "I don't suppose he sang for you? He had one hell of a voice. There was a time when I saw him quite often. Long ago, of course, but if Lalo Molfino had played with him, I'd know it. I find that quite odd."

"I don't know that they did perform together," Jacobo said. "He just said he'd hired him, it could have been for someone else. I don't remember much about him, just the name, the fact that he was husky and wore a tie, and he had a big watch on his wrist. And he came from Lima. An elegant type. I don't know what he was doing in Chiclayo, I just remember him saying the name Lalo Molfino, and I jumped out of my chair when I heard it and told everyone him and me had gone to school together at Santa Margarita here in Puerto Etén."

"Did he tell you anything about what Lalo was up to in Chiclayo? Or was he in Lima by then?"

"He didn't say, and we changed the subject, because no one besides us two knew Lalo," Machado said. "Our talk turned to soccer, if I'm not mistaken."

On the bus to Chiclayo, Toño Azpilcueta thought about this conversation, and about Abanto Morales. He'd heard he was sick. He'd have to find out for certain when he was back in Lima—that would give him a reason to see Cecilia again at the Bransa. She knew the composer, and could tell him if the rumors about his health were true. There was no point in staying around Chiclayo, Toño thought. There was nothing else for him to find there, and he'd be better off taking the Roggero bus back to Lima that same day and skipping the rice with roast duck he'd been looking forward to for days.

On his way home, unable to sleep—he was traveling at night this time, and couldn't see the lonesome deserts or those occasional glimpses of the sea with its roaring waves—Toño thought about his book. He had gotten less out of his visit to Puerto Etén than he'd imagined, but he did gain some insight into the psychology of Lalo Molfino. He'd need to find more people to interview to fill in the gaps. Hopefully Abanto Morales would be one of them. Or should he just invent everything he didn't know about Lalo, turn his book into a kind of novel, a fantasy about the guitarist? No—that wasn't what he wanted. His vision was of something based in rigorous research, based on the truth as he had found it out for himself: *huachafería*, the creole vals, and that little-known figure who had dug a guitar out of the trash, rigged it up, and played on it a music that was the summation of the Peruvian spirit. He would talk about how the vals hadn't existed for three centuries under colonial rule, when the white people of the Peruvian upper classes had their own music, imported from Spain, and the poor, the slaves, had their own music and their own dances, too, many originating in Africa. Those two musical worlds hadn't come together until after independence, well into the nineteenth century.

Toño thought of the past decade, and the fratricidal war in the country that left piles of bodies every day. About what had made the Shining Path overrun those villages lost in the mountains or plant bombs in the cities in the sierra, even in Lima, murdering their fellow citizens. When had the country been ripped in half, tearing the mountains from the coast and brother from brother? Didn't it need a book that would bring it together? The question was whether he could write that book, whether he could capture the Peruvian soul in such a way that all his countrymen would recognize themselves in it and remember the ties that bound them. Toño smiled in the darkness of the bus, feeling a little sorry for himself, and recalled the Peruvian habit of believing that thinking was tantamount to doing. Was it true for him? Was a dream enough for him, a fantasy, or would he capture his ideas in this work that would revitalize the country? He would, he told himself. He had the will, and he had five thousand *soles* to do it with, thanks to Collau. Toño felt certain his book on Lalo Molfino would come into being. He couldn't let his neighbor down.

XII

I would like now to mention Gérard Borras, a young foreigner wise in the ways of our land, whose study *Lima, the Vals and the Creole Song (1900–1936)* I referred to earlier. This author, a member of the French Institute of Andean Studies, addresses, in this rigorously academic text, the brief period when songbooks began to appear—a period he has researched in the greatest depth. In addition to these songbooks themselves, he has examined with a scholar's curiosity the magazine *Variedades*, and he offers a detailed account of the influence of the Peruvian vals in those years when its popularity spread widely among the middle and lower classes. The press and the people of Lima employed the vals, and Peruvian music in general, to memorialize current events, political dealings, and crimes that captured the public's attention, among them the deaths of two famed aviators, Octavio Espinosa and the American Walter Pack, whose planes collided in midair and crashed, killing the pilots and their crews and shocking all of Lima. Entire series of creole songs and valses mourned this occurrence. Those were the early days of aviation in Peru, and men like Espinosa, Carlos Tenaud, and Juan Bielovucic enjoyed great fame. I use this example simply to show that the Peruvian vals wasn't only music: it was also, for many, a source of news.

The vals wasn't the exclusive property of the people of Lima; it was known in the provinces as well, and with its spread, it soon became—and in this way, it was the first of its kind—a truly national music of the people, one that united Peruvians of all stripes. Its early creators were humble: poor people, many on the verge of indigence, workers, stonecutters, bricklayers, street cleaners, lamplighters, quarrymen who scrimped and saved until they could buy a guitar for themselves, or pooled their spare change to give one to a friend. A decisive character in the music's spread was Felipe Pinglo Alva, whose death in 1936 left a void in the hearts of thousands of Peruvians all across the nation, one they struggled but never managed to fill. Even to this day, he remains the lodestar of Peruvian music.

Anything and everything was a fitting topic for a vals, from local goings-on to macabre and even masochistic subjects, such as appear in "The Mouse":

> Roaches and mice
> Refuse to let me dream,
> They creep up on my mattress
> And I wake up and scream.

Or this *tondero*:

> From Lambayeque to Chiclayo
> They slew a *huerequeque*,
> And from his beak they drew
> A mestizo from Lambayeque.

After Felipe Pinglo Alva's death, a beautiful singer with a tremendous voice appeared, Jesús Vásquez from Rímac. Her refined conception of the vals contributed like nothing else to its acceptance among those spheres of society that remained resistant to its charms. Young people brought her their songs, and she brought them to a wider audience on the radio and in the early Peruvian films. Vásquez traveled the world and found success wherever she landed. If she took up much of the limelight, it remains true that many other women made their names during this time: Serafina Quinteras, Amparo Baluarte, Alicia Lizárraga, Estela Alva, La Limeñita, and others. But none of these would achieve the fame of Chabuca Granda, who was the first to truly establish Peruvian music outside the country's borders and find an audience for it around the world.

In 1915, an article in *Variedades* mentioned a duel between two bandits, Tirifilo and Carita, which the latter won. The events were recounted in heroic, even chivalrous tones, and many valses subsequently commemorated the conflict. And then there were the political valses, about the Tacna and Arica campaign in the War of the Pacific and the yearning for the return of these lost territories to Peru, or the wretched war with Colombia, fought in the Amazon—historical events that stoked the country's most noble patriotism. It is strange that the French scholar so meticulously documents these matters, yet finds no room to praise—one supposes he never had the chance to hear him—the immense contribution to creole music made by Lalo Molfino.

XIII

On his return to Lima, Toño Azpilcueta felt the urge to see Toni Lagarde and Lala Solórzano, to have lunch with them and talk about his project. He knew they went out for a walk in their neighborhood every afternoon. They were getting on in years—they must have been around ninety—but they still hadn't lost the habit.

Their conversation began on the topic of Toni's reading. Since his retirement, he'd developed a near-obsession with the history of Peru, and had devoured books by the masters in the field, such as Porras Barrenechea, Jorge Basadre, and Luis E. Valcárcel. These men had come to life in his head, the Hispanists fighting the indigenists, and he still wasn't sure which side he was on. When he cracked open a book by José de la Riva Agüero and fell prey to the enchantments of his prose, with its fin-de-siècle flourishes, he told himself he was a Hispanist, but when he turned to authors from Cuzco, above all Uriel García, he became an incurable indigenist. His ideological changefulness amused him, but it got on everyone else's nerves.

Over their meal, with ample portions of the lady of the house's quince jam, Toño told his friends about the generous loan Collau had given him and his travels in Chiclayo and Puerto Etén. He announced his resolution to write his book about Lalo Molfino and advocate for his ideas about *huachafería*. His friends laughed, seemingly incapable of taking his words seriously. Pretending not to notice, Toño got straight to the point. He wanted to know about the surviving members of La Palizada, if there were any. Toni and Lala weren't sure; much time had passed since they'd seen any of them. They confessed that they hardly listened to Peruvian music on the radio anymore. They'd become addicted to radio dramas, and when they were at home, if they weren't reading, they'd sit snug in front of their receiver to hear the old, extravagant, often bloody tales a station had recently begun rebroadcasting. Lala told Toño that if he wished to write about *huachafería*, he couldn't leave out those entertaining stories, which reminded the couple of the beginnings of their own tumultuous love. Toño wasn't so sure: he doubted that the radio serial was a strictly Peruvian phenomenon, and he found it offensive that the genius of the masters of the vals, the way they pressed their ear to the human soul, should be compared to the hijinks dreamed up by scribblers paid by the job who probably knew nothing about Peru or its people's sensibilities.

Toni laughed at his objections and told him that no matter who the writers for radio were, they had a good idea of Peru's realities. He gave, as an example of the sort of scandals that were their bread and butter, the drama surrounding his own inheritance. This was a matter that had been resolved years ago, but Toni still recalled his siblings' astonishment as they were sitting before the notary and he declared that he wouldn't touch a cent of what he was legally entitled to because he respected his parents' decision to disinherit him following his engagement to Lala Solórzano.

They had protested: after talking, they'd agreed that their parents' last wishes no longer mattered, and they wanted to give their brother what he deserved. But Toni stood his ground. He wouldn't touch what he'd been denied because he'd fallen in love with a girl who was black and poor, and the rest of the family should divide up what was left with no hard feelings (they hardly ever saw each other anyway). The notary arranged things so that the proceedings had a veneer of legality, and when the meeting was over, they all embraced.

With a scholarly air, Toño informed him, "That's a subject for a vals, not a radio drama."

The oldest of Toni's brothers had been a lawyer, the other was a banker, and his sister's second husband was a well-off Chilean residing in Peru. They had properties, though General Velasco had appropriated some of them with the Agrarian Reform Law. They used to invite Toni and Lala to visit, and at times, to keep up appearances, they'd gone, but they were bored in the presence of those big shots and trophy wives who blathered on about *business* and took little to no interest in Peru's history. They showed excessive regard for Lala, to conceal the racism they evidently possessed, and years ago had even proposed she join their music clubs, dance groups, or reading circles. She had agreed for the sake of cordiality, knowing they'd forget her as soon as the soiree had ended. She and Toni got along with his relatives, but only at a distance.

Carmencita Carlota, however, was close to her cousins, and one in particular she'd have over often to eat buns with her mother's legendary preserves. As he heard all this, Toño envied the bond between Toni and Lala. How had they managed it? Toño felt sure the adversity they'd faced in their early days had helped. They'd been stubborn, and it had proved their salvation. And now their love for their daughter had strengthened their bond. He and Matilde made a sorry comparison. They'd come from the same neighborhood, La Perla, and their courtship had aroused no resentment or suspicion, let alone resistance on the part of their families. And yet, they were drifting further and further apart, and bickering and nitpicking were deepening the cracks between them. Creole music, he thought again—that had been the glue that had brought Lala and Toni together across racial and social lines, and there they were now, old and content, keeping each other company. They were a model couple, without a trace of that bitterness that eats away at so many people who have lived together a long time. It didn't take much—just a quick look around—to see how miserable most people were, how they were constantly fighting for wealth and happiness or something else they'd never achieve, while Toni and Lala, too poor to travel the world or even see the sights in their own country, were happy. They wished they could have seen Cuzco—vacations were always out of their reach—but they didn't let it get to them, and there were other things that made up for all they didn't have. Like their love, which allowed them to enjoy a book together, or watch a film, or listen to the radio, to one of those dramas that stirred them and gave them something else to look forward to at ninety years of age, even if Toño found them a little tawdry. They still listened to music, of course, and the sounds of valses and marineras must have made their two bodies move as one in bed, Toño was sure of it. Matilde and he couldn't dream of such a thing. How long had it been since they'd enjoyed lovemaking? The answer was devastating. Months, maybe years. He'd lost track.

There weren't many like Toni and Lala, and he saw in them the proof that his ideas about music were correct: that the revolution the vals was responsible for in their lives should be reproduced far and wide in Peruvian society, bringing people together, putting an end to prejudice, doing away with social barriers. That would be his book's thesis, Toño informed his friends. People tended to take religion, language, or wars as the constituent elements of a country, a society's fundamental realities; it had occurred to no one that a song or music could stand in for these. A mere moment's thought made one realize that music was *the one* art form capable of engendering fraternity, even eroticism. "You're the proof," Toño said, pointing at his friends, and nothing they said could persuade him otherwise. Enthusiastic, he was pontificating aloud, almost yelling, and waving his hands so energetically that the wooden seat beneath him creaked and threatened to break.

Toni and Lala looked at each other, surprised by their friend's vehemence. At one point, Toni interrupted him to say that not all in their lives was as perfect as it seemed, but Toño clenched his jaws and corrected him: "I won't hear that, my friend." He wagged his finger back and forth. "You two are an example. For me, and for the entire country."

They finished their buns with quince jam and Toño told them goodbye, promising them a copy of his book when it was finished. "To two souls, brought together by the vals, who are the pride of this mestizo country, my Peru," the dedication would read.

XIV

The cajon is among Peru's greatest contributions to music. Its origin is lost in the night of centuries, though it must date back to the Spanish conquest, which brought many people of African origin, both free and enslaved, across the Atlantic. The history books say little about the black people who accompanied the conquistadors, beginning with Christopher Columbus, though we know they were already in Peru by the end of the fifteenth century and participated in the destruction of Tahuantinsuyo, the Inca Empire. In those remote times, black people made up as much as a third of the crews on Spanish expeditions to Peru, and slaves who showed great bravery or extraordinary diligence were often granted freedom in return. The historian Porras Barrenechea notes that, despite the censoriousness of the Inquisition, African music and dance made inroads into the population from the country's earliest days. Many of the black people who came to Peru were Muslims who had converted to Catholicism in Spain, and their original faith exercised an influence on that mingling of races and cultures that gave rise to the Peruvian people. Some of the oldest photos taken here show musical groups in which the cajon and its player are given pride of place.

The cajon is a symbol of poverty, the instrument of

people too poor to buy a harmonica, let alone a vihuela or a guitar. Like a shadow, this instrument they invented accompanied the marineras, valses, and *huainitos*, and all the other music created in this country that conspired to emancipate itself from foreign rule, finally achieving this when General José de San Martín sailed north from Chile and laid siege to the Spanish in Lima, beginning a process that would culminate in Peru's independence in 1821. The inventor of this instrument is lost to history, though scholars must be right in attributing to it an origin among the people of African descent present in the earliest Peruvian bands and orchestras. Its origins are humble, of course; its function of marking rhythm represents, perhaps, the oldest musical impulse. Its name, an augmentative of the Spanish word for "box," hints that it likely made a virtue of necessity—that its prototype may have been an ordinary crate repurposed for the making of music. Those who know prefer cajones of aged hardwoods—cedar or birch. These give it a better tone, and are more obedient to the percussionist's hand. Nowadays, music shops sell brand-name cajones, which, you may imagine, dear reader, are not exactly optimal, and often sound worse than the battered instruments of street buskers. The rhythm of the cajon is bewitching. Spaniards who traveled to Lima from Andalusia fell in love with it, and took it back to Spain, where it has become, along with castanets and the guitar, an essential element of the flamenco music characteristic of that country's south. Or so, at least, my worldly musician friends tell me.

Now that the sound of the cajon is familiar worldwide, many countries lay claim to its invention. But about this there can be no debate: much to our credit, the birthplace of the cajon is Peru. Its greatest virtuosos live here, in Lima, on the coast, in the mountains, even in the jungle, and our music wouldn't be the same without it. There is a special savor, a kind of soul to the cajon's music, as though the spirit of the wood were speaking through it. Without its perfume of the Amazon, of its plants and exotic trees, the marinera, the polka, the vals wouldn't be the same. And any veteran will tell you, the older the instrument, the better. Some of these seasoned players will hold on to their instruments until they literally fall to pieces.

A true cajon player will have weathered, calloused hands, a good ear, and a voice that can more or less stay on key. Nowadays, there are music schools and conservatories that teach the instrument, but people still say the best players learn by ear, by performing on the street. They never seem to miss a beat, and I can attest to the beauty and resonance of their performances. These men, often illiterate but experts with their palms and fingers, bring life to the vals and the marinera, and singers will tell you their presence is obligatory. I said "men"—and many of the best players, who are as one with their instruments, are men—but in Lima, in Andalusia, and elsewhere, there are women whose elegance and timing give the fellows a run for their money.

Allow me the pleasure of a brief inventory of the most celebrated players in Lima—some well-known from the groups they perform with, others virtually unknown. Among the latter I would count the father of Lala Solórzano, Juanito Solórzano, who was rumored to be a maestro and who, until his death from old age at nearly one hundred, dazzled with his instrument in the backstreet of Mirones where he lived in tight quarters with a gaggle of grandchildren, great-grandchildren, and others.

Or Cojo Lañas . . . might any of my readers ever have heard him play? Throughout his life, he received offers from bands looking to recruit him, but he always turned them down. A true bohemian, he drops in irregularly at clubs when he knows a group he likes is coming round, and without warning, he hops onstage and works his magic. My god: what hands and what an ear. He's a man of negligible stature, had polio when he was a kid, but when he plays the cajon, he grows and grows and seems to levitate over the crowd. He reminds me of a Lalo Molfino of the cajon. Everyone's given up on trying to hire him. The bands just show up for their dates and hope this storied figure will one day bless them with his presence.

And I can't fail to allude to another magnificent cajon player: Carlos "Caitro" Soto, a majestic player who used to accompany Chabuca Granda on her tours overseas.

I have mentioned already *El Waltz y el valse criollo* by César Santa Cruz Gamarra, whose sister Victoria was a famed choreographer and scholar of Afro-Peruvian folklore. In this book, he states that the three great Peruvian cajon players of the fifties were Francisco Monserrate, Víctor "The Hook" Arciniega, and Juan Manuel Córdova, also known as "The Kid from Piura," a master of *tonderos*. These percussionists appeared frequently on the radio, and almost always ended with a marinera or a *tondero*. Santa Cruz Gamarra goes on to attribute to the singer and composer Yolanda Vigil, beautifully nicknamed "La Peruana," the credit for bringing creole music to a wider audience in Lima during her concert at the Embassy Club, and doing so with all the seductive vivacity the women of the coast are known for. It was she, Santa Cruz Gamarra claims, who broke the barriers of the back alleys, seeding the fever for creole music in the rest of Peru.

Far be it from me to question the wisdom of the illustrious Santa Cruz Gamarra, but I believe this happened earlier, with the widespread acceptance of the cajon and its players, as well as the radio, to which the author seems not entirely well disposed. Indeed, he is rather contemptuous of the medium, appearing to think that the vals lost something of its quality and original character as it spread through all layers of society. I, of course, disagree, and believe that the rupture of the strictures holding our music in its place was the best thing that could happen to us as a country, helping Peruvians of all classes to recognize themselves as one people in those songs.

César Santa Cruz Gamarra became a well-known figure in our country, first as a composer and musician. Born into a talented middle-class family, he spent his childhood in La Victoria in Lima. I have mentioned his sister Victoria, whose books, articles, and lectures were instrumental in illuminating many aspects of Peruvian popular culture, and the family also included singers, dancers, a bullfighter, a playwright, and an inventor.

I would like, though, to close this chapter with a brief homage to César's brother, Nicomedes, an esteemed versifier or, more precisely, a *decimero*, an improviser of *décimas*, poems whose form dates back to the Spanish Golden Age. The versifying tradition developed in Peru in the colonial period, but its exact history remains unclear. Nicomedes overcame the prejudices he faced as a black man to revive and popularize the art. Often, he recited poems written beforehand, adapting them to the circumstances, but at times, he would draw on his surroundings to extemporize stanzas of true brilliance. I saw him in public once or twice, and heard him on the radio, and I admired his ingenuity, his unforgettable, deeply personal style, the way he could pull applause from an audience. At the height of his fame in Peru, he traveled to Spain to popularize his country's music and verse, finding, perhaps, fewer admirers there than at home, however well-regarded he was when he died in 1992. There was no one else like him, and I ask myself whether he suffered in Spain, where the echoes of his native shores could no longer reach him. Let us bow our heads in reverence now and show him the respect that eluded him in Madrid.

XV

Toño Azpilcueta worked all week on his book, taking breaks from sorting the information he'd discovered about Lalo Molfino and speculating as to the whereabouts of Abanto Morales only long enough to teach a few music and drawing classes at the Colegio del Pilar.

Then Cecilia Barraza cleared things up for him. The Abanto that Jacobo Machado had told him about had nothing to do with the musician from Cajabamba. Abanto was the other guy's *first* name, not his family name, and he'd just happened to hear Lalo playing, and he was swept away by fantasies of making a mint by starting a creole band. Abanto was a businessman, he couldn't carry a tune in a bucket, he was clueless about music, but he knew a good racket when he smelled it. He'd once worked in the transport business in Chiclayo, to the north. Now he was dealing in seafood in the port city of Callao, not far from Lima, where Toño found him.

"I've been trying to find you for days," Toño told him when Abanto received him in his tiny office near the port. "I imagine you'll want to know why I was so insistent about talking to you. It seems you had the good fortune to know the finest guitarist Peru ever produced, one Lalo Molfino, and as it happens I'm writing a book about him in the hope of doing justice to his talents. I'm hoping you'll tell me a bit about him. Anything and everything you can remember."

Abanto looked at him with disappointment. He must have hoped Toño was looking to propose some sort of business deal—anything but dropping in to remind him of some musician he hadn't seen in ages.

"I curse the day I got mixed up in the whole creole music racket," he exclaimed. "Because of that Lalo character, we never put on a single show. He was miserable, a son of a bitch if you ask me, with all kinds of weird demands and obsessions. He said he had to play alone—he didn't want to be a part of any band. Because of him, all the musicians I hired quit. I'd shelled out for them to rehearse, I basically pampered them, I even bribed them to get them to make nice with Lalo, but they all threw in the towel. He was a rat, a real bastard, that Lalo Molfino."

That tore at Toño's heart, and he nearly shouted at Abanto; he was as offended as if those comments had been made about himself; but then he recalled that he'd heard all this before. It was hard for him to accept, though, and he refused to believe it for the simple reason that things just couldn't be that way. The genius behind a music so fraternal, so full of love, could never be an individualist, let alone a narcissist so disdainful of other musicians that he refused to even share the stage with them. Toño had seen the magical effects of his guitar playing—he had felt them in his bones. That night in Abajo el Puente, he'd wanted to hug the audience, kiss his neighbors, he'd have emptied his pockets for any of them. Lalo's music had made them his brothers and sisters. Those chords and notes were Peru's silver and gold cast out to the audience in generous handfuls.

And so, he thought, there had to be some other explanation for what Abanto was telling him.

Feeling he'd made a mistake in chasing Abanto down, Toño said it was best that he go. But then the businessman said something that changed his entire perspective.

"The one person who could stand him was this girl he was in love with. She was very thin, quite young, she used to come around for him in the evenings. I don't remember her name anymore. Maluenda. Something like that."

"Lalo had a girlfriend?" Toño asked, surprised.

"Yeah. Poor thing," Abanto reminisced. "I remember them walking off holding hands. She'd come for him when practice was done. You should talk to Miguelito, he was the cajonist, he'll remember her better than I do. We used to drive the truck together, now he makes fishmeal for me at the factory. He's a solid worker."

Tense, Toño took down this Miguelito's information and hurried back to the National Library to add a few lines to his essay. He was pleased that he'd learned something important about Lalo Molfino, but still irked by the crude and dismissive way Abanto had spoken of him. He was sure people were missing something about Lalo, the same way he had been wrong in the past when passing judgment on great artists. Toño recognized that he'd been unfair; a lack of perspective could lead one to draw rash, sometimes uninformed conclusions. Hadn't there been a time when he had been dismissive of the great Chabuca Granda?

Chabuca hadn't believed it, but Toño was glad so many people in so many cities all over the world had admired and embraced her work. But when he first heard her valses and pasillos, he wrote, in more than one article, that her lyrics expressed a fantasy, not the reality of Lima's colonial past. That elegant Lima of hers, half-Andalusian and half-Arabian, where horsemen in ponchos of fine linen, gentlemen, and beautiful and distinguished young ladies strolled over the Suspiros Bridge or on the Paseo de Aguas on the other side of the river, or rolled in the aromatic yellow flowers of the Pampa de Amancaes—had that place ever really existed? Or was it simply an invention, like certain of those traditions described by that old romantic, Ricardo Palma, that obscured and transformed Peru's reality instead of revealing it?

As Chabuca Granda seduced massive audiences inside and outside of Peru, garnering fans of the Peruvian vals as far away as Chile, Ecuador, Colombia, Argentina, México, and even Brazil, Toño Azpilcueta had dared object to the version of the Peruvian past her songs put forward. "If only the great Felipe Pinglo Alva had been so famous!" he blurted out in a concert hall one night, causing an uproar that led to an interminable argument.

In his articles, and when he'd spoken to her in person, he had been more respectful. He'd had no intention of insulting someone who had brought such success to his country's music. He did have his doubts, though, about those moving moments in Amancaes that kept showing up in her music: were they real, and was it really handsome young men and gorgeous society girls from Lima who had taken to the vals so readily, or was it, rather, the humbler people, unshod, unperfumed? Toño felt it necessary to assert that the vals's origins weren't aristocratic, that it had been the poor and hungry masses who had given birth to it—only later had it escaped the alleyways to make it into the living rooms of the middle classes, and then, years later, the finer sort of people had finally caught on to its charms.

Quite some time after one of his articles about her was published, Toño had been invited to appear on a program with Chabuca Granda on Radio América. He asked her a question that irritated her, and she gave him a stern look and refused to answer. This was one of the most embarrassing moments in Toño Azpilcueta's life. Happily, their quarrel never made the rounds of the gossip press, so the wider public knew nothing of it. Her prestige continued to grow, and with time, Toño's opinion of her changed. So what if the Peru she evoked had never existed? It did now, thanks to her. Were artists obliged to be true to history as it happened? Had other great musicians of the past been faithful to history? Of course not—Mozart and Wagner had invented a mythological past far more extravagant than Chabuca's colonial Lima, but their work had survived thanks to their originality and the strength of their talent.

She deserved praise rather than criticism. Inventing this past had made her a true creator, and her verses were real now that they had lodged in the minds of hundreds, thousands, perhaps millions of people who knew by heart those valses and pasillos that were the artistic embodiment of Chabuca's dreams.

Toño had renounced his old views in print, but Chabuca never forgave him, and whenever they saw each other at a concert hall or show, she had always greeted him coolly, glacially even. To err is human, and he had erred with Chabuca, and so perhaps Abanto and José Durand Flores and even Cecilia Barraza had misinterpreted Lalo Molfino's behavior. A virtuoso of his kind couldn't be as selfish, rude, and insensitive as they had described. Not when his music was the very opposite of all that. Toño's book would show the truth, but first he needed to find that skinny girl—a native of Chiclayo, he imagined—a girl who had known how to read Lalo's heart.

XVI

The death of Carlos Gardel in 1935 in an airplane accident in Colombia was a catastrophe for the world and for Peru. Known, because of the beauty of his voice, as "El Zorzal" (the song thrush), he had brought fame to the tango across the globe, aided by the growing reputation of Argentina (it goes without saying, those were different days). In Paris, this versatile dance for two took on a peculiar form popular among street gangs: the Apache tango. Couples in other countries added their own touches, too.

The tragedy of Gardel's death only added to the tango's popularity. In Peru, it slowly pushed the vals aside. J. Chávez Sánchez's text entitled *Tangomania*, widely read in Lima, described the phenomenon thus:

> The boys from Malambo must be fools,
> Bucking and kicking like rowdy mules,
> The marinera's style and grace
> They've lost in thrall to the tango craze.

El Cancionero de Lima, a monthly magazine and songbook, published a full-page article, which some deemed in bad taste, with a headline that read: "Carlos Gardel, Widely Revered, Died Singing the Tango 'Going Down.'"

The ensuing tango fever caused Felipe Pinglo Alva and the singers of the Old Guard to react patriotically, blocking the Charrúa path down which popular tastes had begun to roll, to the displeasure of the neo-Indian soul so beautifully portrayed by that portentous mind from Cuzco, José Uriel García. These men used their talents and wits to put the tango in its place and restore the popularity of the vals as the nation's music.

This is yet another feather in the cap of the humble men of that generation—mestizos, dandies of a kind, not just Pinglo but also Pedro Bocanegra, Carlos Saco, Víctor Correa Márquez, Manuel Covarrubias, Filomeno Ormeño, David Suárez Gavidia, Nicolás Wetzell, Alberto Condemarín, and Luis de la Cuba. I doubt they knew they were changing the face of Peru, let alone that from a cultural and musical point of view they were, in a certain sense, giving birth to it. There, in the narrow alleyways, in the poor and working-class neighborhoods of Lima—Mercedarios, Barrios Altos, Rímac, Malambo, Chirimoyo, and a hundred others—they drank pisco and chicha and sang, danced, and played the guitar for up to three days on end. They died young, lungs ravaged, of yellow fever, smallpox, malaria, or tuberculosis. They were heroes, and they never knew it.

The vals, of Spanish or Austrian origin, or perhaps both, engendered dances in Chile and Argentina as well as in Peru. But it was only in Peru that *huachafería* appeared: an exaggeration of sentiment, a verbal styling, that I believe to be Peru's most significant contribution to world culture. At its zenith, *huachafería* produced true poetry, as in *The Black Heralds* of César Vallejo; but it is no less present in the endless cast of children filing through the verses of José María

Eguren, who seems to have grown up among Scandinavian faeries; and we mustn't fail to recall the bombast, like an adman's pitch, of José Santos Chocano, crowned in Lima's town square like the heroes of ancient Greece in an unforgettable ceremony that was itself the embodiment of *huachafería*. This phenomenon united whites, mestizos, and Indians thanks to the universal popularity of the vals.

Felipe Pinglo Alva epitomized this trait, this phenomenon, this essence of the Peruvian character, and he granted it immortality in his dedication to the Peruvian vals, unflagging despite the tuberculosis that slowly devoured him. This admirable bard was well aware of what he was doing; in a letter, he spoke of his "determination to create a national music." This commitment, perhaps, was what drove him to forgo a more superficial style, peppered with commonplaces, in favor of more serious themes, some even encroaching on the perilous terrain of politics. Think, for example, of "The Commoner," with its invocations of injustice that even today rend listeners' hearts.

His chosen subject was love, but he didn't flee the muck and grime, and he saw clearly the misery, the deprivation, the injustices the poor were made to suffer, as well as the hopes of the boys and girls of the middle classes, who dreamed of happiness and conquering the world. "The Poet of the Paupers," they called him, and scholars have increasingly paid attention to a critical period between 1924 and 1926 in which his songs not only attained a previously unknown artistic excellence and poetic originality, but also revealed deep social sensitivity and a passion for denunciation that never lost the subtle elegance characteristic of his lyrics.

His life was sad: rich but cut short by tuberculosis, to which he succumbed at just thirty-seven years of age. In that time, he composed three hundred valses, or likely more. His parents, Felipe Pinglo Meneses and Florinda Alva Casas, died young, and he was raised by his aunts, Gregoria and Ventura, who pampered and indulged him and exercised a profound influence upon him. He was educated at that signal institution of Peruvian life, the Colegio Nuestra Señora de Guadalupe, and his name will be forever associated with Barrios Altos, where he lived for much of his life. He eventually found work as a secretary in the War Ministry in the infantry department. Clearly the roar of exploding gunfire didn't diminish his sensitive spirit.

Witnesses unanimously describe him as a small, thin man, attentive and amiable, above all with women. He would step away from the bar or table at two in the morning, or three at the latest, declaring that he must work the next day.

Recognition came to him late, arriving only after his death, and was never, perhaps, in proportion to his greatness. Some knew his name thanks to his work on the radio or the soundtracks of such early Peruvian films as *The Rooster in My Shed*. But most of his recordings were made available only after his death, because Lima long lacked factories capable of pressing records for mass distribution.

I admit there is something in his lyrics that irks me at times: his prostration before the lofty female figure. In "The Commoner," there is a plaintive and, if you will, classist note. That line about "loving an aristocratic woman / a commoner like himself . . ." Is this taking for granted the prejudice and racism of Peruvian society not a tacit manner of accepting it?

At any rate, I would just as soon the "whites" and "Indians," as we call them, vanish, swallowed up by a campaign of total miscegenation. Already, the vals and creole music in general have made their contribution, encouraging all to mingle with all to produce the mongrel nation that will reveal Peru's truest essence. This mixed Peru, indelibly impure, is already present in the country's music, in the guitar, the cajon, the jawbone, the cornet, the piano, the lute. Its harbinger was the vals, with all its *huachafería* and mawkishness included, clarion of a country free of racial prejudice, as envisioned by the great intellectual José Uriel García.

XVII

Dear Maluenda:

At last I've found you. Let me assure you, it hasn't been easy. I've been searching for more than three weeks. I tell you this not to burden you with my complaints, but rather to give you some sense of my dedication. I found you thanks to Miguel Cuadra, an employee of Abanto in Callao, who was briefly a music promoter and discovered a guitarist as near to my heart as to yours: the illustrious Lalo Molfino. Don't be startled, I beg you. Abanto informed me that Miguel had been a friend of yours and of Lalo's, and added, with the greatest respect for your privacy, that you and Lalo were quite close, and that he presumed the two of you were in love. This is why I have sought you out, and I will explain everything to you just as I did to the good-natured Miguel Cuadra.

My name is Toño Azpilcueta, and I am a writer on creole music—a critic, some would say a pen pusher, scribbling articles on artistic goings-on in Peru. I believe my work aims at something greater: I would call myself a seismograph measuring the intensity of the vibrations of the nation's soul. And believe me, I have never noticed such shock waves as in the presence of Lalo Molfino. I experienced the miracle in person only once, but that event sufficed to sow eternal gratitude in my heart as well as a deep interest in his talent and cast of mind. In many bars, on many street corners, I've seen the guitar shine, but nothing has ever compared to that evening when Lalo took the stage in Abajo el Puente. I was so struck that I have decided to dedicate a book to him. And it is here that I would like to invite you to make your entrance, my friend.

Please don't be alarmed. The purpose of these lines is simply to beg for your priceless testimony. You must be the person who knew Lalo best, who was closest to the sacred vessel of his soul from which those divine chords emerged. Do not fear for your reputation: unless you wish otherwise, your name will not appear in my book. Nor will I disregard your wishes as concerns your testimony. I am writing this work in the certainty that Lalo Molfino was the most original and extraordinary talent Peruvian music has ever seen. You and I both know it, but the people don't, and it's for them that I am writing, that they may learn of this genius God took away from us too soon.

Allow me, please, to invite you to breakfast at the Bransa on the Plaza de Armas this coming Monday. The buns there are delicious—I doubt you'll soon forget them. If you cannot come on Monday, I'll be there on Tuesday and Wednesday as well, waiting for you. I ask you with all my heart to come: for a conversation, nothing more.

Cordially,

Toño Azpilcueta

Will she come? Toño asked himself, sitting at the Bransa with his cup of chamomile tea. In the end, she did: not on Monday or Tuesday, but on Wednesday, looking tentative, nudging the door to the café open with her feet. Toño had grown tired of waiting, and had more or less lost hope. As soon as he saw her on the patio, his heart sped up. *It's her,* he told himself.

Maluenda was dressed so poorly that the waiters took her for a beggar and tried to throw her out. Toño jumped between them, taking her arm and telling them, "The lady's with me." He guided her to his table and pulled out a chair for her. She was wearing a thin blue overcoat that looked very old—*She must be freezing in it,* he thought. Her shoes looked like house slippers, her feet were swollen from much walking, and her toes, with twisted, unpainted nails, were exposed. She looked terrified. Toño asked her, "What would you like? Those buns I mentioned, with mountain cheese? A café con leche, maybe?"

The woman nodded silently. She looked young, but there was also something timeless in her features. She was nervous, glancing around at times with a frightened expression. While her face was pretty, the abandonment in her eyes gave him a sense of foreboding.

"I appreciate you coming," Toño said with a smile. "As you can imagine, without your help, my book would be a pretty sorry affair. You know, I had no idea that Lalo Molfino had a lover right here in Lima."

She nodded again, but didn't smile, and then Toño heard her voice for the first time: "I don't know why I came, sir. I don't know what I'm doing here." She looked, not at Toño, but just past him.

Toño ordered for her, and only once her stomach was full and she saw that this stranger was happy to treat her to anything she desired did Maluenda lower her guard.

"I don't know if Lalo loved me," she confessed, pressing her finger into the plate to retrieve the fallen crumbs of her bun.

Their relationship hadn't started romantically. It was more direct, more spontaneous than that. Lalo would see her leaving the café where she worked, which was close to the bar where he and Miguel Cuadra used to practice with a few others. One day, he decided to talk to her. He did the same another day, and on the third, he took her by the arm and dragged her off despite her protests, the blows she rained down on him, and her threats to call the police. Lalo kissed her. Then he let her go. Maluenda ran a few steps away, then stopped and continued walking. Lalo came up beside her and escorted her to her home on the Avenida Sáenz Peña without a word. By way of goodbye, he kissed her again, this time without resistance, on the mouth, with saliva. She felt his hungry tongue on her thin, timid lips, and she was scared at first, but then she noticed a certain timidity in Lalo. The following encounters were the same: he was impetuous, aggressive at first, but as soon as they'd kissed, he'd look down, lost in thought. He was incapable of expressing affection, and a time would come when he wouldn't embrace her, cuddle her, give her kisses on the neck unless she encouraged him.

"It never went any further than that," she said. "Maybe he didn't love me, maybe he didn't like me enough."

"You only ever kissed? That was all?" Toño asked, his surprise getting the better of his discretion.

Lalo took her back to his rented room in La Perla, a room that had never been cleaned, where all he had was a change of clothes and that guitar, which he tended to the way some people tend to a pet dog or kitten. He spent hours tuning the instrument, not bothering to utter a word to her, bowing his head close to the strings, as though they were speaking to him in a whisper, communicating their secrets. She had taken a liking to him, she'd hinted to him that she was his, that he could do whatever he liked with her. But Lalo did nothing. All he did was talk to her about Puerto Etén, Father Molfino, and the trash heap where he found his guitar.

"People who love each other do things," Maluenda reflected, chewing a bun from their second order, which had just arrived.

The second time he took her to his room, they kissed passionately and caressed each other, and she could see that Lalo was ready. They lay in bed, and she pulled up her dress, lowered her panties, and arched her back, expectant. As she lay there with her hands on her breasts, Lalo stood up and turned around.

"There was something stopping him, I don't know what, but it seemed like he would die of fear. He was happy, and then it was like he remembered someone or something, and he looked away, almost as if my body disgusted him. I never understood, and I never tried anything again. I thought eventually he would take the initiative. But it never went anywhere. A kiss, a squeeze, maybe, that was it."

Toño thought to himself that Lalo must have been the loneliest person he'd ever known of. He couldn't imagine that the thin girl sitting across from him now, washing down her breakfast with coffee, had failed to awaken his interest or his sympathy. There had to be something more there, an inhibition, one probably linked to things he had suffered in childhood.

"How'd you break up?" he asked.

"It was simple," Maluenda said. And for the first time that morning, she smiled. "One day I went to find him at practice, the way I did every afternoon, and Abanto told me he'd fired him because Lalo couldn't get along with the rest of the group. I went to La Perla, and he wasn't in his room. I never saw him again, and I never thought about him until I got that letter from you. I needed someone to read it to me—I can't read, you know. I mean, I can, but not well, it takes a lot out of me. And then I couldn't decide whether to accept the invitation. I hope I won't regret it."

"You won't regret it," Toño said. "My word's good. I won't include anything you don't agree to, and if you don't want your name in the book, it won't be there. Anyway, I don't know your last name, and I don't need to, if that makes you feel better."

When they were done talking, Toño accompanied her to the door and watched her disappear between the cars and trucks parked along Lima's town square. He imagined her passing the cathedral, where the alleged remains of Francisco Pizarro were kept, though they'd turned out to be the bones of llamas and vicuñas. Lalo Molfino's tale was so complicated and so mysterious that Toño realized he might have to do as the custodians of those bones had done: mingle the fragments imparted to him by Pedro Caballero, Abanto, and Maluenda with the bones of some beast from the Andes to produce something resembling a life.

XVIII

An incomparable piece of Peruvian folk culture is the vals entitled "Ódiame," in which a gallant begs his beloved to abhor him, to hate him, in the belief that "only what you've loved may you detest." It's an old song with music by Rafael Otero, and it's likely no one would ever have known the author of its lyrics had Eduardo Mazzini not revealed him to be none other than the great poet from Tacna, Federico Barreto (1862–1929), a man famed for his ferocious poems and articles written to denounce the Chilean occupation of his beloved hometown, which lasted for many years after the War of the Pacific.

I doubt there was anyone more pleased with this discovery than myself, as the volume of poetry in which those verses appear was among the few heirlooms my mother's family held on to. It was dedicated to a friend of my grandmother's who was herself from Tacna, and the poet had sent it to her, along with a love letter, when she was still quite young.

Researchers have spilled a fair bit of ink discussing the alterations to the poem made by Otero or whoever first claimed these lyrics to adapt them to the music. It's generally agreed that these changes were misguided, and that the original text was perfectly suited to musical performance.

The alterations aren't radical, in any case: the first and last lines are a bit different, and the final verse substitutes a hendecasyllable for something the experts call an "arrhythmic dodecasyllable." We shall quote here from the lyrics by which this vals ever was and ever shall be known:

Hate me, please, I beg you,
Hate me merciless, hate me true.
I'd rather be hated than ignored,
To be forgotten stings worse than to be abhorred.

If you hate me, I'll forever know
There was a time when you loved me so.
Hatred harbored follows love professed,
And only what you've loved may you detest.

What matters your pride, what matters my disgrace,
What matters your elegance and comely face?
What good will all this vanity be for
When in grave clothes we lie still forevermore?

The title of the aforementioned book by Barreto was *Something of Mine*, and few copies seem to have been printed, though I do remember studying him in school, so it's unsurprising that people weren't aware of Barreto's relationship to the more famous vals. This friend of my grandmother's whom Barreto was in love with was quite a looker, to judge from portraits of the time (most of them painted, as photography was nearly unknown in Peru at the time). My grandmother was said to be a beauty as well—though since she died the year of my birth, I can't speak from experience. It seems both ladies captured the heart of the great poet, now ignored and forgotten by contemporary tastemakers, who showed great courage, as a poet and journalist, in the face of the Chilean oppressors but was eventually forced to leave Tacna for exile in France, where he died in Marseille in 1929. He was buried there, and no one places flowers on his grave on the Day of the Dead.

Evidently, this is the text of a love poem, but its beginning is disconcerting: the lover begs his beloved to hate him. Charming as it may be when set to music, there is something philosophical taking place here of great interest: in the speaker's moment of delusion, hatred is the residue of exhausted love, and he holds on to it because he finds consolation in those bitter ashes. It's sad—deep down, we Peruvians are a sad people—and yet there is something soothing in this belief that "only what you've loved may you detest."

This is one of dozens or perhaps hundreds of examples of the speculative thread that runs through the vals, nourished by thinkers who studied the human soul in depth and transmitted their doctrine through music. "Ódiame" gives the lie to that cliché of creole music as joy, as light amusement. It has a metaphysical substrate, an undersoil of sorrow and pain, bitterness and melancholy.

But there is an even better example, perhaps, of these tendencies I'm speaking of: a vals that confronts death, absorbs death into itself, one that takes place in a cemetery and reaches a dramatic conclusion. I am speaking of "The Caretaker":

> I beg you, caretaker, when I'm gone,
> Hide all traces of my humble tomb;

Tear the ivy from the lawn
And let no flowers bloom.

When I die, may all forget me
Because my life is at an end.
Let no mourner's prayers upset me,
Do me this last favor, friend.

Tamp down the earth where I sleep,
And if my woeful beloved calls,
Let her not stand above me and weep:
Cast her out past the graveyard's walls!

It is this last verse that touches me most deeply, that exclamation at the end, that command: "Cast her out!" It is the bitter summation of those lamentations that rise up like the soil on a grave mound through the preceding lines, marking the progress from love toward death as the culmination of existence. More than a few valses contain such beguiling meditations on death. Eduardo Mazzini, whom I've cited earlier, attributes the authorship of these words—a fine example of what he called the "deep and philosophical inclinations" of the music he studied—to the Colombian poet Julio Flórez (1867–1923). It matters little, or perhaps not at all, that this author was not Peruvian: his poem likely has little significance among his countrymen, but it has become an indelible part of the culture in Peru, where it remains popular to this day as the encapsulation of a morbid and masochistic streak in our national character that I will return to in later pages.

XIX

That night, Toño could barely sleep. An idea took hold in his mind, something he'd only suspected before but was now certain of: Lalo Molfino must have known he'd been abandoned in a trash heap in Puerto Etén. Toño imagined the memory pecking away at his soul like a ravenous bird. It explained everything: his lack of descendants, his horror of sex, which for him must have meant, first and foremost, the gestation of children whose horrified mothers would abandon them in the mire to be eaten by rats. It was dreadful to think a place as small as Puerto Etén had harbored such awful secrets. Toño imagined Father Molfino arriving in the village with that foundling; imagined the people there seeing him, the wagging tongues speculating that the boy must be his, the more astute among the townspeople putting two and two together and realizing Lalo was an orphan. He imagined the children at Santa Margarita, cruel the way children can be, telling Lalo during a soccer game at recess: "Lalo, you're garbage, the priest found you in the dump." The very thought of copulation, of the process that could engender such a tragedy, had grown disgusting to him, to the point that he couldn't bear the thought of being inside a woman. These notions tormented Toño, and when he finally got to sleep, his nightmares were once again plagued by pestilent rats.

Toño awoke with the same thoughts in his head. Did Lalo's knowledge of his origins explain his need to stand tall above others, as if to redeem himself from his tragic past? The poor boy. Toño examined the pages he'd written. Should he revise them now in light of what Maluenda had told him? He wasn't sure, and for the next few days, every time he sat down to write, he felt paralyzed. He told himself he needed more information, that there were still secrets in Lalo's life waiting to be revealed. He thought of Lalo's irritability, his desire to stand on the stage alone, which everyone who had tried to hire him had spoken of . . . Was it the knowledge that he'd once been defenseless, that he'd have died had it not been for the charity of an Italian priest, that compelled him to tell himself he'd never need anybody again? Considering his own life, and imagining himself a famous author in the future, Toño wondered what would happen if someone took an interest in his biography and began rooting around in his past. Might such a person discover a secret that he himself didn't know? That the Italian immigrant with the Basque surname wasn't his biological father, that he'd adopted him, for example, or lifted him from a trash bin in some alleyway in Lima . . . This speculation made Toño chuckle nervously as unease crept through his entire body, and he had to stop writing and walk outside for a breath of air.

On nights when he knew he wouldn't sleep, Toño liked to stay up late talking with Collau. His friend never asked him about the progress of his book, but he listened quietly as Toño spoke to him of what he'd learned as the two of them (or three, when Matilde came out, too) sat under the lamppost on their block. When he described Lalo's revulsion to sex, Collau agreed with him that the musician's origins had to have something to do with it.

"Dammit, you're right! It scared him," Collau said. "If he got the little girl pregnant, the whole thing would have come back to him. Who could get it up with something like that on his mind?"

"It probably made him play prettier," Matilde added. "He reserved all of his attention for the guitar."

Collau burst out laughing. "He got his rocks off stroking his instrument," he said, shaking his head.

Toño's dreams that night were repulsive, obscene, and he woke with a feeling of disgust. He wrote for several hours before Matilde came to tell him breakfast was ready. He hadn't felt the time passing, hadn't hesitated at any moment, his pencil had glided relentlessly across the many pages of his notebook he filled. Thankfully free from the stomach pains that ordinarily plagued him early in the day, he looked over what he'd written as he drank his herbal tea. He corrected a few things, but for the most part, he was happy with what he'd done. He washed quickly, dropped his two daughters off at school, giving each of them a kiss, and traveled on to the National Library. He would continue writing there until lunchtime, when he would eat the sandwich that Matilde prepared and wrapped in a napkin for him each day. The waiters at the Bransa allowed him to sit at one of their tables while he ate.

The librarians had already put aside all those fifty-year-old songbooks for him, but that morning he just flipped through the pages, barely reading or not at all, turning over and over in his mind Lalo's struggles with intimacy. Considering what was missing in his writing, he came to feel that Matilde was right: Lalo's talent was the compensation for his sufferings. And so his story, his book, would have to begin in horror: with the night Father Molfino went to administer extreme unction to a dying woman and heard a cry that led him to discover a newborn boy just before he was eaten by vermin. He would then work toward the other great theme of his essay: *huachafería*. He would separate the two themes at first, letting many pages pass before they merged in a marvelous embrace. He had seen great writers work this way; now he would, too. What was indispensable, though, was to come up with a title, even a provisional one—he could change it later, that was fine, he had a feeling he wouldn't know definitively until he'd reached the end. He could see the chapters clearly now, one after another.

That week, he finished a draft of the first part, entitled "Apprenticeship." It told the story of Lalo's discovery of the guitar in Puerto Etén, how he restored the battered instrument, how he learned to play it. He became acquainted with creole music—through Chabuca Granda, of course, her song "José Antonio," which he thought was popular when Lalo was a boy. Later, Toño would revise everything and make sure the facts lined up.

He told Collau and Matilde that night that he'd filled an entire notebook with a prologue and several chapters. He was happy, and his wife and friend noticed, remarking that they'd never seen him so euphoric. He spent an entire week like that, writing morning, noon, and night, and on

Sunday, he read through all that he had written. Then, feeling content, deeply satisfied, even, he carefully tore all his notebooks into tiny pieces. He would have to change everything. The book would instead have an anodyne beginning, kids playing soccer, a ball rolling across a field, a boy sending it flying with his head. Lalo Molfino would be there, sympathetic, lively. Then someone would tell him where he'd come from. The story would move backward from that point to Father Molfino giving Domitila her last rites.

He spent a few days on this new version and informed Collau and his wife one night that now his book had truly taken off and the wind was in his sails. Again, they remarked on how pleased he seemed, if a little overexcited. The next day, he tore everything into pieces once more and dropped them into his wastebasket. He started over with his dialogue with Maluenda at a table in the Bransa. He would explain early on that Lalo suffered from a sexual trauma. A revelation like that would trap readers right at the start. From his intimate wound, everything would unfold: the guitar, his experiences at school; only at the very end of the book, with a wealth of detail, would he recount Lalo's sordid beginnings.

Toño's fascination with his subject didn't flag, and each night, Collau and Matilde listened to him patiently, respectfully, nodding along as he rambled in yet another fit of euphoria, sensing already that once more, he would tear up his work and start over, and not understanding why. But Toño knew. He was searching for the perfect way to begin his book, which he knew would be the first and last he wrote, despite his many years as a critic and scholar; he was sure that he would finish it and die, exhausted, of stomach cancer or something like that, leaving those pages behind for Matilde and Collau to publish when he was gone. The book would appear posthumously, when the worms would already be eating him, unless he were cremated—how much would that cost? He didn't want Matilde to have to go on paying for him even after he was gone—but of course, the book would be a great success. Not initially: it would first make inroads among the "intellectuals," who would recognize Toño Azpilcueta's great talent, the originality of his ideas, the brilliance of his theories on the origins of the Peruvian national character, the importance of mestizos in the country's history, his message about unity in diversity. All this would come across in time to the music of Lalo Molfino, the poet, that extraordinary guitarist who took up his instrument by chance and out of nowhere became the symbol of everything Toño wished to express. Toño Azpilcueta was happy.

A week later, when he reread what he had written, he remained satisfied, even felt blessed, and yet again he tore all he'd composed into tiny pieces. He had made a new decision: the first chapters of his book would contain his thoughts on Peru itself, on the vals, on *huachafería*. He would start with a description of the Lima that nearly disappeared with the War of the Pacific, the brutality of the occupying military powers, the sieges, the ferocity with which that then-small but rebellious city was whipped into submission, the books stolen from the National Library, later recovered from across the world by the scholar and maniacal letter writer Ricardo Palma. Then the wars waged against the Chileans from the Sierra by General Cáceres with his makeshift army of hill dwellers and mestizos. It was in the midst of all this that the real Peru was born—the Peru of the vals, of *huachafería*—in Lima's poor neighborhoods of Chirimoyo and Malambo with its winding streets, in La Palizada and on the fields of Amancaes, in parties that lasted two or three days, in Felipe Pinglo Alva and all those other impenitent guitarists whose lives ended too soon, ravaged by unsanitary living conditions, by poverty and disease.

He decided to read a few pages of this new version to Matilde and Collau, but no sooner had he started, under that flickering lamppost, than he regretted it. His ideas had changed, and he left his wife and his poor friend disconcerted as he stopped, telling them he'd realized that the truth was that he hadn't begun his book at all. The months he'd spent working hadn't been in vain, because he was certain now that his was a worthy project, and that he would rewrite everything once more, but better. Toño said this, and he believed it.

The next day, he started over on the first page, with clear ideas about the proper way to tell the story of the elusive life of Lalo Molfino, accompanied by a major essay on the culture and customs of Peru. He labored another week, with not a thought for money or life's demands, and Matilde worked her magic so that he, Azucena, and María could eat on what little she made washing and ironing clothes. She was working more than ever, because, since starting his book, Toño Azpilcueta had given up writing the articles that helped supplement his meager salary from the school.

"Why do you tear up so many notebooks, compadre?" Collau asked him one night. "Don't you like what you write?"

"I do. A lot. Every day I write better than the day before,

I'm certain of it," Toño told him. "It's just that it's hard for me to find the beginning, the point I can move forward from."

Matilde said nothing. She'd never seen her husband so concentrated on one thing. Their daughters noticed, too. They told their mother, "Dad's really enjoying what he's doing. He seems like a different guy, like he's changed skin, the way a snake does. He's never been so happy in his life."

Over and over, Toño kept trying. And a day came when he realized that he'd done nothing for a year but jot down his thoughts about Lalo Molfino, *huachafería*, Peru. He knew what he was doing. For once, his book was moving in the right direction. What he read was beautiful, captivating, accomplished. Feeling proud of himself, he gathered his courage and invited Cecilia Barraza to breakfast at the Bransa. To pay, he needed to ask Matilde for a couple of *soles*. She gave them to him without asking questions.

XX

If creole music owes an homage to one man, it's Óscar Avilés. Chabuca Granda is rumored to have said, "If it wasn't for Óscar Avilés, Peruvian music would be dead." And that is true. He's a great guitarist and a great singer, a tireless man who adores creole music and uplifts the spirits of his friends, ever ready to help them polish their lyrics or instrumentation, or to stand in for a fellow musician who's fallen sick or is off traveling.

Chabuca Granda didn't only champion him, she idolized him, as every Peruvian who believes in our music should. I share her enthusiasm, and I consider Óscar Avilés one of the eminent creole musicians of our time. He was born in Zepita, a neighborhood in Callao, the spoiled son of José Avilés Cáceres, a notable photographer and pioneer of Peruvian cinema. At twenty, Óscar made the choice to play professionally, and since that time he's hardly put down his guitar. His music has a highly personal quality that he describes in this way: "When I began playing, the accompaniment stuck to the lower register. I had the idea of trying high notes. And that's the style now associated with my name." Connoisseurs will know what he's talking about.

He's known, as I've said, as the "first guitarist of Peru," and I would call him that as well, were it not for Lalo

Molfino. But he is certainly the person who's worked hardest to make creole music a genuine expression of the Peruvian people, an art that at once portrays them and gives them a voice. He accomplished this with some of Peru's most storied players, from Los Morochucos to Fiesta Criolla, a band founded in 1956, as well as the Dávalos brothers, Rosita and Alejandro Ascoy, Zambo Cavero, and many others I will forgo naming because life is short and the list would be endless.

The greatest achievement that can be ascribed to Avilés, perhaps, is his role as a promoter of Peru's music. No one has encouraged more young people to form bands of their own, and no one worked harder to raise their spirits when they were faced with the indifference or contempt of the masses. Chabuca Granda said that if it hadn't been for Óscar Avilés, she would never have recorded her album *Dialogando* in Argentina. This compilation of her own songs was her stepping stone to international fame.

Though I'm unsure how old Óscar Avilés is now, a quick glance at the high points of his creative odyssey makes it clear that he must be far along in years. But you wouldn't know it if you saw him tuning up or stepping out onto the stage. Even in his heavier days, he was always impeccably dressed, his trademark mustache trimmed to the millimeter at a precise distance between his nose and upper lip. He's the first to arrive at a performance and the last to leave, as everyone knows, and will happily lend a hand to anyone, from young upstarts to his contemporaries to the old veterans ready to retire. His discretion is the stuff of legend—next to nothing is known of his family or his private life. When he has spoken of others, it has been most often with his trademark generosity, as in his oft-repeated praise of Chabuca Granda: "Chabuca sang about things we all love. She was an eminent songwriter, but an eminent composer, too."

For these and many other reasons, I beg of all those touched in some way or other by creole music—writers, practitioners, enthusiasts—to pay homage to Óscar Avilés, so long as he lives. It is long overdue, and there is no one who deserves it more. This is a question not of magnanimity but of justice, and I imagine his eyes will fill with tears as he receives his due words of praise because—let's be honest—he's a creole through and through, in other words, a Peruvian sentimentalist.

XXI

Cecilia Barraza walked into the Bransa at ten in the morning on the dot. A broad smile on her face, she kissed Toño on the cheek and gave him a hug. He was pleased to see her, his friend, his secret love, as beautiful and elegant as ever. She was wearing a pale dress and a new-looking raincoat, her hair was styled, her perfume was aromatic, and she was impossible to ignore with those graceful, beaming eyes.

"You're a hard man to find these days, Toño," she said with a smirk. "I've been asking everyone what's become of you. They say you're working on a book. Is it the one on Lalo Molfino?"

"It is, and it's progressing quite nicely," Toño replied. "I just need a title. I was thinking about *A Nip of Champagne, Brother?* But I'm not sure. That's a nod to my friend Collau, who ran out of his house with a bottle when they collared that son of a bitch Abimael Guzmán. 'A nip of champagne, brother?' he said. And in that moment, I had a revelation: those five words contained everything I wanted to say, the feeling, the spirit I want the book to have."

"I don't know," Cecilia said, frowning. "A nip of champagne, brother? It sounds like the punchline to a joke."

"Not at all," Toño replied, very serious. "It says it all: fraternity, festivity, unity—there's a sensibility expressed in it, a way of looking at the world. The emotional bedrock of the valses we love so much."

"I've missed you, Toño," Cecilia said with a grin, leaning over and hugging him once more. "I've been looking for you all over. And you want to know why I've missed you? I believe you're the only friend I have. The only real friend, I mean, because there are no hidden romantic motives here, no seduction, no undeclared love."

Toño's expression was affable, but his heart froze in his chest. He felt as if Cecilia had plunged a dagger into his entrails. That declaration of friendship caused his happiness at being with her to crumble, destroyed the secret dreams he had of her as his queen.

"You're my closest friend, too," Toño said. "I was just about to tell you so. That's how we manage to go on loving each other without ever fighting: we're close friends and nothing more."

"There you have it, brother," Cecilia agreed. "Now, tell me a little about this book of yours."

Toño told her all that she didn't know about Lalo Molfino. About Maluenda, about Lalo's inability to make love, about his theory that linked Lalo's traumatic birth and rescue from the rubbish heap to his love for the guitar. Then he made the leap to *huachafería* and his thesis, the very core of his book: that it was this quality that had given birth to Peru as a nation, that had determined its personality.

Cecilia Barraza took her time absorbing his words, then responded, "I'm afraid I'm not convinced. *Huachafería* may be a trait of some Peruvians, but not all of us. I don't think it's characteristic of me. Or my friends and relatives. Or of you, Toño."

"You're wrong there, and I'm quite proud to admit it. *Huachafería* is our one great contribution to world culture, and I'm going to prove it in my book!" Toño sounded exalted. "When you read it, you'll see that I'm right."

"I don't know, Toño. I think you're barking up the wrong tree," Cecilia said. "But don't pay me any mind. Maybe your book will convince me in the end."

She quickly changed the subject to her tours in the Peruvian interior and outside the country. She was exhausted, she said. All year, she hadn't stopped. Invitations to perform at festivals had poured in from all over Latin America, and for the most part, she had accepted them. Now, though, she was tired, and she'd booked a passage on a ship, telling no one where she was going, because she needed rest. "I don't suppose you'll mind, Toño, if I don't tell you either." Despite her exertions, she was struggling to sleep and had lost several pounds. On her thin frame, it showed.

"This has never happened to me before," she continued. "I've always slept like a baby. But now I lie down drained and I can't close my eyes all night. This vacation will do me good. At least I hope it will."

Toño turned over in his mind the question of Cecilia's relation, or lack thereof, to *huachafería*. Maybe she was right and it was irrelevant to her. Maybe that explained a lack of elegance, of spontaneity in her valses and polkas. Did that, then, refute what Toño wished to say about Peru and Peruvians? He would have to think it over sincerely.

He and Cecilia talked another half hour and agreed to see each other more often, once a week, at least. Too much time had passed, they both agreed. She insisted on paying, telling Toño he could treat her after he'd published his book, which she was sure would find countless readers.

Watching her depart, airy and merry as ever, Toño felt depressed. She was the love of his life, she was leaving, and she had confirmed that there would never be anything between them. Good friends. How those two words stung.

But after a few minutes passed, he was once more submerged in his writing. Cecilia was wrong, he told himself—at least about him. *Huachafería* lay in his very bones. If she couldn't see it, if she failed to understand something so basic about him, then they weren't made for each other. Recognizing this calmed him down. It was better this way, perhaps. At least he wouldn't waste his time fantasizing about a relationship that was impossible.

He went to the library and worked without respite for several hours. He arrived home late, but chose not to go inside, preferring to sit under the lamppost writing all night, keeping his eyes peeled for any rats lurking in the ditch or the bushes. He even prepared his classes for the next day. Then he dragged Collau, Matilde, and Gertrudis out, gathering them in the scant light to listen to him rave once more. They listened very respectfully as he ranged from the vals to subjects as remote as the Spanish viceroys, unsure how they should respond. He explained that his book might have contradictions, that Lalo Molfino and all he represented might recede into the background as Toño tried to draw in other questions, such as Catholicism and the Spanish language. They were disconcerted; they didn't understand; and they thought that too much time in the library had made Toño's mind stray into the unfamiliar.

The book was taking shape, but in places it was bursting

at the seams, and here and there were excessive leaps and yawning lacunae. Lalo Molfino was becoming a pretext to talk about any and everything, whatever might conceivably prove relevant to Peruvians. One day, Matilde, who generally woke earlier than Toño to prepare his breakfast, approached him, her face looking haggard.

"I'm sorry, Toño, but I can't do this anymore," she said. "I've tried up to now not to bother you, I've worked harder to bring in a few more *soles* and to hold our home together. But it's over. I'm tired, I'm afraid I'll get sick, and I worry about our daughters. What will they do if something happens to me? You need to start writing again—articles, I mean, things you earn a check for. It may not be much, but we need it badly. I know you're underpaid, I know sometimes you don't get paid at all, but we need everything we can get. I can't do it alone anymore. I'm sorry, Toño."

Her eyes were glistening, and he thought a few tears would spill out, but she managed to hold herself together. Toño quickly told her she was right. He hadn't been conscious of the situation before that day. He would go back to writing those articles, of course he would. He would go back to putting his expertise in creole music to good use, would do interviews, would chronicle the important happenings in the music world. And everything he earned, he would turn over to Matilde. He didn't mind. What he wouldn't do, though, was take time away from his book. He would burn the candle at both ends. His sleep would suffer, but he would write. He had several dozen pages now. He could feel the book beginning to be born.

XXII

After taking Peruvian vals all over the world, Chabuca Granda died in a hospital in Florida. The surgeons there did what they could, but it was no use. When her remains were sent back to Peru, her compatriots, this author included, paid homage to her as she deserved, and masses of us accompanied her mortal remains, grieving but full of admiration and reverence for this master composer and singer who brought such happiness to all of us who love our music as she did.

Thousands of people paid their respects at her coffin, thousands more in the cemetery where she was laid to rest; they revered her, and they ached at the thought of a life without her presence. A statue was raised in the memory of the composer of "El puente y la alameda," "José Antonio," "La flor de la canela," and those hundreds of other songs that can now be heard from Tokyo to Paris, from Buenos Aires to New York.

It merits mention here that unlike so many composers of valses, polkas, marineras, and all those other styles that make up our nation's music, Chabuca emerged, not from the humbler classes, but from the upper crust of Peruvian society, from an elite family that nevertheless proudly proclaimed their regard for the music of their homeland.

Chabuca was taught from an early age to love the guitar and popular melodies, and she showed promise when she was just a girl, soon revealing an incomparable gift for songwriting. Her voice found disciples and faithful fans from all corners of the world, and it is thanks to her that Peru's folk music is played in town squares and parties on five continents. No one did as much for our music, and no one else gave such time and respect to the country's poor, who revealed to her the secrets of the Peruvian vals.

Though famous as a daughter of Lima, Chabuca was born in the Sierra, in Cotabambas, Apurímac, in 1920. There are photos of her on the banks of Lake Cochasayhuas with her parents in 1922 or '23. She was briefly married, and had three children, to whom she dedicated many songs: Eduardo, Teresa, and Carlos Fuller Granda.

Here I must make a confession, about something I regret every single day. I spoke with her once on Radio América on the occasion of a prize she had received, and though I was and remain her admirer, I dared to ask her about the origins of those stories from her valses and *tonderos*, the pretty society girls walking along the Paseo de Aguas in colonial times, surrounded by gentlemen from the finest families. After all, the vals, and Peruvian music in general, had been typical of the lower classes, the mestizos, the poor, whom the aristocracy had repudiated, treating the art of creole music with maximum disdain.

Chabuca Granda didn't care for what I'd said, and now I wish I hadn't bothered. It was, moreover, a rather stupid remark. Worse still, I wrote a flippant article in which I repeated these criticisms. Why shouldn't a woman of the upper class embrace popular traditions? Why shouldn't she have molded them to her own experience? That mingling of the vals and the marinera with those images of high society, men in fine straw hats riding walking horses on the far shores of the Rímac River, stirred the heart of many a young girl. They were lovely compositions, and it was natural that Chabuca's valses should idealize the colony that had existed three hundred years ago, using images of it to lend charm and beauty to the country's music. What I'd expressed was a prejudice, and in music, there should be no prejudice. This is a lesson that I learned from the great Chabuca. Let the upper classes take part in our nation's folk culture if they will. Songbooks aren't history books, and their authors can add or subtract what they like; the lyrics will live on based on the stories they tell, even if it's pure invention.

I understood that late, and I regret what I said; I uttered it in bad taste, in the presence of Chabuca Granda herself. I will repeat here: I have nothing but admiration for the achievements of this woman who made of our vals a music the entire world could take part in. She lived too few years, she left us too soon, as happens with the great artists, but still: so long as the Peruvian vals exists, Chabuca Granda will live on. And so I declare now, like all of Peru: long live Chabuca Granda, the great!

XXIII

Toño Azpilcueta got up early, while the last stars still shone in the sky and a fringe of dawn was creeping into the darkness. He sat under the lamppost and began revising his long manuscript. What he read surprised him. Everything he had wanted to say about Lalo Molfino and the transformation of Peru through creole music was there. Attentively, he studied his own words about the guitarist from Puerto Etén. He could say no more, he realized, because he knew no more.

His considerations on Peru took up three-fourths of the book, and he felt they were well integrated, from the Inca Empire down to the political strife of the present day. The rise of Tahuantinsuyo, its days of glory and decline and the war between the brothers Atahualpa and Huáscar, the arrival of the conquistadors from Spain, which changed everything, the rebellion of those peoples subsumed by the Inca Empire and the imposition of the so-called white people who, on the basis of their alleged superiority, had governed Peru ever since . . . Spanish was there, too, the linguistic marvel, tongue of Cervantes, which had little by little changed the destiny of the peoples of Latin America, bringing them mutual understanding after a thousand years of strife and conflict worsened by the infinite languages and dialects spoken across the continent.

The civil wars followed, then the long yawn of three centuries of colonial life: Saint Rose of Lima and Saint Martín de Porres, endless saints and endless processions, the Inquisition, the viceroyalty, San Marcos—the first university in the Americas—convents, seminaries, church after church, and rivalries among the conquistadors themselves. The colony ended, the republic began, with military coups and caudillos in rapid succession, until Peru became a country diminished and torn by vast divisions between its peoples: between speakers of Spanish and Quechua and the other regional languages, between the prosperous and poor—the insignificant minority of the very rich and the masses who live in misery.

Then came the champions of the Old Guard, Felipe Pinglo Alva with them, to revolutionize this country in decline, to bring order through a music that united all Peruvians and transformed their society, inciting an entire generation of creators, people brought together not by their race but by their originality, who helped forge a modern, dynamic Peru that would at last be the envy of Latin America.

The book was done, Toño realized. He spent that day and the remainder of the week carefully reading its two hundred pages in the National Library. He made corrections, emendations, but found nothing essential that needed changing. At last, he kept telling himself, the book was done. It contained everything he'd wanted to see in it. Tired, almost dizzy, he had to accept the bittersweet knowledge—not so much knowledge as a feeling, a feeling less of celebration than of weariness and infinite fatigue—that he was done. He recalled his long period of work, during which he'd never really believed the day would come when he would revise it, jot down a few notes, and set it aside.

Toño wrote by hand. Before submitting his work to a publisher, he would need a clean version of the text. Meek, ashamed, he asked Matilde to lend him the money to pay a typist. A few weeks later, he held two copies in his hands. He took them to the library and read them again. He corrected a few typos, but apart from that, he found his work even better than he had before. He had chosen for a title *Lalo Molfino and the Silent Revolution*. It didn't entirely convince him—he retained great affection for *A Nip of Champagne, Brother?*—but it contained the kernel of what he'd written about.

He informed Collau that at last he was done. Collau was happy for him, and, rational soul that he was, his friend turned immediately to practicalities: "Now, Toño, it's time to find a publisher."

Both men underestimated the time and effort that would take. They first wrote Planeta and Alfaguara, the largest publishers in the country. Both responded within a week, praising the book to the skies, but apologizing that they had no room for such an essay in their catalogue. Given the unusual topic, they doubted sales would suffice to justify publication, and they advised Toño to keep looking.

But Lima wasn't exactly brimming with publishers, and Toño fell victim to frustration. He told himself that neither those first two publishers nor the others he had written to understood the range of his book. When it triumphed, they would regret their shortsightedness. He tried smaller publishers affiliated with bookstores. They read his manuscript, sent him their affectionate regards, had kind words for his talents, but declared that Toño's book was utterly out of step with what was currently fashionable among the country's readers. It wouldn't sell, they explained, and so they couldn't risk publishing it, at least not yet—but hopefully, tastes would change and they would have the chance to in the future.

Toño had not counted on such unanimous rejection. Saying nothing about it to Matilde and Collau, he placed his copies of the manuscript in his suitcase and decided to stop trying for the moment. He was tired, fed up, disgusted at the realization that he'd worked so hard on a book no one wished to publish.

That was when the miracle occurred. A letter arrived, addressed to him care of the National Library, and was duly handed over by one of the clerks there. Its author, a Mr. Antenor Cabada, wrote that he had heard of Toño's "interesting work" and that, after a lifetime as a bookseller, he now had ambitions of becoming a publisher. He wanted to read Toño's book; if it was to his liking, he would bring it out. And he asked Toño to send him a copy at his earliest convenience, please. Toño clutched the miraculous letter tightly, hardly able to speak. He soon called this Antenor Cabada, who greeted him effusively and repeated everything he'd said in his letter. Toño hurried out to send him the manuscript, and the former bookseller, having read it, told him in another conversation on the phone that he was prepared to publish it.

They spoke for a long time about the cover. Mr. Cabada agreed to hire an artist from Lima to design it. Afterward, they decided on the typeface. Within a month, Toño had his first copies in hand. Stroking those pages of slightly coarse paper, Toño was surprised to find that the book that had cost him so much effort brought him neither joy nor a feeling of triumph. If anything, he felt a sort of resignation. The tension, the expectation, were gone. His mission in life was fulfilled; in its absence, he was utterly empty. He felt sad, and spent hours staring at the meager volume. It seemed a lie that he had worked on it so long.

Cabada told him the book would be distributed in the few bookstores in Lima and throughout Peru. Toño should take a stroll, he said, so he would see it in the display cases. He took his publisher's suggestion, but his book was nowhere to be seen. It didn't occur to him that this might be because all copies had been sold. He was not even pleased to hear that Cabada had spoken with the Ministry of Education, which had offered its auditorium, free of charge, for the presentation. Toño agreed to speak there, to save Cabada the worry of finding some reputed intellectual to stand in for him; still, Cabada convinced Rigoberto Puértolas, an older but very lucid scholar, a former president of the federation of primary and secondary school teachers, to join them. Puértolas was retired, but he'd remained active on the intellectual scene and continued to hold sway among the people in his field. Since Toño insisted on presenting the book, Puértolas would give the introduction.

Over the next two weeks, there were no reactions on the part of critics or readers, but Cabada insisted that Toño's work was being read and discussed, particularly his analysis of Peru's history and contemporary reality. On the night of the presentation, Toño washed and shaved, and he arrived at the auditorium in the Ministry of Education at seven forty-five, fifteen minutes early, in a carefully ironed jacket and tie. The room was immense and desolate, with fourteen or fifteen attendees at most, the majority of them old people who had come in seeking shelter from the cold. It was the dead of winter, and at that hour, the winds were numbing all across Lima. Collau, Gertrudis, and Matilde, who had bought herself a new dress for the occasion, sat in the front row. They were excited to see him mount the stage and sit at the center of a table with his publisher and Rigoberto Puértolas, who was older than Toño had thought and seemed not to know what he was going to say.

Toño was frustrated. He'd prepared a fine speech, which he would now read to a mostly empty room. Puértolas, distractedly shaking his hand, looked around as if unsure of where he was or whom he was talking to, and struggled to read the words he'd scrawled on a sheet of paper, which he had to hold very close to his eyes. His voice was soft as he pronounced Toño's name, described him as a great promoter of creole music, and affirmed that readers would surely know him from his many articles on Peruvian folk culture in the press. And now he had published a book, Puértolas said—he stuttered as he pronounced the title, *Lalo Molfino and the Silent Revolution*—and all over Lima and in the rest of Peru, it had provoked intense discussions of its affirmations about the nation's character. Toño had, moreover, revealed in it the existence of an eminent, and unfortunately deceased, Peruvian guitarist, who in his short life had left an indelible mark on creole culture. There was no applause when he finished, and to Toño's and Cabada's surprise, Puértolas then left the stage, walking slowly and tapping his cane audibly on the floor, producing strange echoes in the rows of the empty auditorium as he departed.

Toño waited for the door to close behind him before taking out his index cards, preparing to address the scant group before him. None of the editors or directors of the magazines he wrote for were in attendance. He tried not to lose heart, though he couldn't help but think that everything he had to say he could have said in Villa El Salvador, on one of those warm nights he liked to spend with his wife and neighbors, who were sitting by themselves in front of him, waiting for him to speak.

Toño had never addressed such a group in a setting like this, so grandiose and so empty, but he imagined all those seats filled with readers hungry for his words. He spoke of his mentor, the great Hermógenes A. Morones; smiled as he recalled learning that the *A* of his middle name stood for Artajerjes; he must have hated that name, Toño thought, which he'd likely been given in honor of some distant relative. Morones had held a professorship in Peruvian studies at San Marcos—alas, the position was no more—and Toño mentioned his encyclopedic knowledge, the studies he'd carried out with no help from anyone across the vast territories of Peru, the articles he'd written, the books that revealed, for those who had taken the time to read them, Peru's rich and varied popular culture, especially in the field of music.

Toño recalled how, as a young man, a boy even, still in school, he had taken an interest in his country's music and, with no one to guide him, had begun reading and writing about the players and composers largely ignored by the upper classes, people who delighted their ample public in Lima and the provinces with that music that the hero of his book, Lalo Molfino—whom he'd only seen once—had taken to its highest expression. He spoke of the spell he'd fallen under the night Durand Flores had invited him to Abajo el Puente, of the sound of the guitar strings plucked by the kid from Chiclayo (or from Puerto Etén, more precisely), even of the gleam of his patent leather shoes, the sight of which was somehow inseparable from the sounds produced by his prodigious playing.

Discreetly, Toño spoke of the revolution he hoped Peru's music, especially the vals, would bring about; and of its extraordinary composers and instrumentalists, singers and revelers, beginning with the Old Guard who had initiated it. They had transformed Peru from the ground up, he affirmed, reigniting a greatness not known since the Inca Empire, one based not on imposing temples and palaces and wars of conquest, but on the mingling of races, classes, and cultures to give birth to a people without complexes or prejudices; and slowly, Toño predicted, this society would come together in such a way that no one was beneath consideration and all were treated as worthy human beings. Progress and respect would reign, and Peru would become a model for the rest of Latin America. He chose not to speak of *huachafería*, but he did mention the arrest of Abimael Guzmán and the decline of violence, which represented an opportunity for music to foment a spirit of fraternity that would forever unite the Peruvian nation.

Three people—the three he already knew, who had come from Villa El Salvador to see him—applauded enthusiastically. The oldsters, bundled up to keep out the chill and nodding off, followed suit, but less fervently than his wife and friends. He thanked everyone and stood. Cabada congratulated him with a hug. He felt a flash of pride as he saw the gleam of tears in the old bookseller's eyes.

On his way home in a taxi, Collau's treat, Matilde said the one thing they were all thinking: what a shame it was that more people hadn't attended, because Toño's presentation had been splendid. The others agreed.

The next day, not a single line about the event appeared in the newspapers. Nor were there any mentions of it in the magazines Toño wrote for, apart from a brief but enthusiastic little article in *Folklore Nacional*, but even that was muddled, the author evidently not having made it past the first chapter of the book. His publisher told him that his book shared the fate of virtually everything published in Peru, but for Toño, this was no consolation. His inevitable frustration convoked the rats, which came forth to pester him at night; he would awaken from his nightmares terrified, struggling not to rouse Matilde as he lay there hoping for sleep to return.

XXIV

What sort of music did the Incas play? Did they have time for music, with their constant conquests expanding their frontiers and incorporating new peoples into Tahuantinsuyo? It is doubtful, particularly when we recall that the empire endured only a hundred years before dissolving amid internecine conflicts and the misguided feud between the Ecuadorian Huáscar and the Cuzcan Atahualpa.

Their ancestors had been a cautious people who preferred persuasion to aggression, and their conquests proceeded tranquilly prior to the arrival of the Spanish. But the division of the empire between Cuzco and Quito covered the Andes with corpses. Moreover, the peoples the Incas had presumed subjugated—the Chancas and the Huancas among them—soon rebelled against their masters in ways that would favor the Spanish, signaling the end of the Inca Empire.

Again, did Incan music and dance exist in these times of conquest, of assimilation of so many people into Tahuantinsuyo? They must have: martial music and dances intended to teach these peoples to obey. Collective movements rather than aesthetic ones, artistic expressions proper to a warrior people, utterly unlike the Inti Raymi celebrated nowadays, when thousands gather in Cuzco once a year to frolic, chant, and drink.

Colonial rule in Peru, for the three centuries that it lasted, failed to unite and integrate society with its saints, its Masses, its religious ceremonies and processions. The nobility and the upper classes were ignorant of the enormous indigenous population, despite exercising absolute authority over them through the army and the smaller local militias created to break the natives, punishing them cruelly, attempting to pacify them through repression and fear. And though the Inquisition here burned relatively few at the stake—just seven people in three centuries, according to a Chilean specialist on the subject—it was always there to remind Peruvians that they could be sent to the flames if they got out of line.

The priests and clerics were there to cultivate "the true religion." And the fanatical enemies of idolatry stole and mutilated thousands upon thousands of sacred objects and statues of the Inca gods, which were numberless, as the Incas incorporated into their pantheon the deities of all the peoples brought into their fold.

Naturally, three centuries could not pass free of indigenous revolts. The most important was that of the chieftain Túpac Amaru II, who led a rebellion of the southern Indians and the Bolivian peasantry. This followed earlier struggles waged in the 1500s, not against the king of Spain, but against the Spanish landowners and the brutal conditions they permitted in the haciendas. The Indians took for granted that the king of Spain knew nothing of these abuses and supported their cause. The landowners, in turn, were opposed to the king, refusing to accept the "New Laws"—more humane than the existing ones—that the crown promulgated, and so they rebelled, with bloody battles ensuing. In the end, the wealthy colonists succeeded in forcing these New Laws' abrogation, and everything returned to the way it had been before. Had this not happened, the colonial Americas might have been a less violent, even magnanimous place. But what conquest was ever kind? In North America it was worse—the outright extermination of the indigenous population.

There were many other rebellions of lesser significance, and more we never have learned of, as word of them wouldn't have reached the cities. These were crushed cruelly, and on the latifundios, the blood of hundreds or thousands of natives was surely spilled in sacrifice to Spanish rapine.

None of this, curiously, is reflected in the music of the time. The upper classes and the minuscule Peruvian aristocracy sang and danced to Spanish music, while the indigenous people played their sad tunes on the charango or something like it, on the cornet, maybe on the guitar. It was not just the affluent who were cut off from the poor, but the mountain people from those of the coast, where the marinera was born. Peru's music developed in parallel, its various strands never touching, until, at the end of the nineteenth century and the beginning of the twentieth, those luminaries whose memory I evoke in these pages brought them together in the music of one nation.

XXV

Toño returned to his routine: research at the National Library followed by a brief walk to the Bransa, where he would have the sandwich Matilde had prepared for him while drinking an espresso with a dash of milk as he wrote his articles or glanced back through that morning's notes. But one day, recollecting his student years with nostalgia, he took the Avenida Abancay to University Park. The University of San Marcos, where he had studied in the School of Arts and Letters, used to offer classes in law, literature, and education near there. Now, all the departments had moved to the corner of the Avenida Universitaria or to the Avenida Venezuela, where Toño had never even been. In the park, he stared for a moment at the building where he'd studied, the halls of which were now reserved for visiting dignitaries, ceremonies, and doctoral defenses. As though guided by an invisible hand, he found himself on the Avenida Nicolás de Piérola, popularly known as La Colmena. He took a table at the Palermo, one of the oldest cafés there. As a student, he'd gone there many times, and he'd been told the poets of the fifties—Paco Bendezú, Pablo Guevara, Wáshington Delgado—had frequented it as well.

He had just sat down and ordered a café con leche when he heard his name spoken. He turned, but saw no one addressing him. Instead, it was two people talking at the next table over.

"Yes, Toño Azpilcueta's his name," a gentleman with deep-set eyes repeated. Well dressed in a vest and sporting several rings on his fingers, he looked like a lawyer. His companion, younger and without a necktie, Toño assumed was one of his assistants. "You haven't read him?"

"Not yet," the young man admitted. "Is he worth it?"

Toño was dumbstruck. The silence and indifference that had greeted his book had wounded him, and now, here he was, by chance, seated next to two men who were discussing it.

"Very much so. I mean, I must tell you, I think the author's not quite got all his marbles. Imagine thinking creole music is going to bring this entire country together, all these different races and languages and ethnicities. Think about the rifts that have torn this country apart and imagine a vals or a *huainito* healing the wounds . . . it's a little much, no?"

"I'll have to read it," the younger man said. "I've got a soft spot for silly romantic notions. It's a nice idea, no? A country united by creole music. I'll have a look."

"You're still a kid, that's why you fall for utopian nonsense. Me, I find it funny. Just think, mestizos, the mountain people, the whites all holding hands and swaying while some joker plays a guitar. Be honest with me: Would you marry some Indian chick who doesn't even bathe and her pussy and ass reek like a pigsty?"

"Screw that," the younger man said with a laugh. "There's a couple of mixed breeds, though, I wouldn't kick out of the sack. I've seen some with bodies you wouldn't believe. Anyway, I'll check the book out."

"At one point, the author says, 'Marx and José Carlos Mariátegui were wrong: the revolution won't be led by those who seize the means of production, but by composers of valses and marineras.' Sure, buddy. I'll lend you the book if you want, though. *Lalo Molfino and the Silent Revolution*, it's called."

"It clearly left an impression on you," the younger man replied. "You keep complaining, but you can't stop talking about it. Who is this Toño Azpilcueta, anyway?"

"He's a writer of some kind. Or a journalist, I guess. Kind of a hanger-on. Not anybody well known."

"What kind of name is that, Toño Azpilcueta? European? Maybe it's a pseudonym? A nickname?"

"No idea. He's a weird one, though, I'll tell you that. One minute he's writing about music, the next he's carrying on about rats. He's got an obsession with rodents. A phobia."

"You keep piquing my curiosity."

"Yeah, well, we should get back to work," the older man responded, motioning to the waiter to bring their check. "Life can't be all fun and games. Remind me to give you the book when we get back to the office, my copy's there."

The two men argued over the bill, and in the end, each paid half.

As they stood, Toño stared at the elegant old man, who looked unsettlingly familiar. He felt the old itching on his calves, the filthy paws of rodents, and to calm himself down, he ordered a second café con leche. It arrived hot, and he drank it in tiny sips, his exasperation growing as he heard repeated in his mind the old man's declarations about the absurdity of his book. But there was another sensation there, too, a kind of satisfaction, an unexpected euphoria, at the thought that he'd been deemed a madman. It was a harsh judgment, a cruel one, but the discussion he'd overheard was proof that his book hadn't met with indifference. He knew now that someone had read it and was talking about it. He wondered how it had sold. Probably badly, but he would phone Antenor Cabada that very afternoon and see. He would drop in on Toni Lagarde and Lala, too, to tell them the story and to give them an autographed copy, which he hadn't gotten around to yet. "Not quite got all his marbles" . . . Did people even say that anymore? It sounded like a phrase from half a century ago. Anyway, better to be known as crazy than not to be known at all. As he departed the Palermo, he no longer itched, and all thoughts of mice and rats were gone. He was pleased: people were talking about him. Maybe just two idiots, but it was a start. His book was making its way. It would arrive in the hands of more discerning readers soon enough.

XXVI

Huachafería is a Peruvian term of dubious origin. The distinguished linguist Martha Hildebrandt, in her book *Peruanismos*, quotes two authors from the magazine *Actualidades*, Enrique Carrillo and Clemente Palma, to the effect that a related word, *huachafita*, derives from the Colombian *guachafita*, meaning "uproar" or "racket." These men attribute the contemporary notion of *huachafería* to Jorge Miota, a journalist and author of stories born in 1871 who contributed to *Actualidades* as well. It is said that Miota first used the adjectival form *huachafo* in its pages in the early twentieth century. Miota was a traveler who lived for a time in Buenos Aires and in Paris, so it is hypothesized that he may have heard the word *guachafita* in Venezuela in reference to a kind of raucous party and imported it from there to Peru, where it became a fashionable term for gaudy to-dos attended by tawdry, ostentatious ladies.

But Hildebrandt recounts a story in her book that gives weight to the thesis of a Colombian origin, one she heard from professor and historian Estuardo Núñez. Apparently, a humble couple from Colombia arrived in Lima around 1890 and took their lodgings on a street near the Fort of Santa Catalina. They had two boisterous daughters who held lively parties attended by their neighbors and, in particular, by soldiers from the fort. This family referred to these get-togethers as *guachafas*. But the locals found this hard to pronounce and began referring to them as the *huachafas*, swallowing the initial *g*, as is so commonly done in Spanish. Though the girls were hardly wealthy, they attempted to appear otherwise, and this led to the term acquiring a connotation of bad taste and tawdriness.

Núñez's sources for the story were his grandmother, who had to put up with the racket from these parties, and his father, who was an army officer and attended these events occasionally with his colleagues from the fort. How trustworthy all this is therefore remains uncertain. At the least, we will attribute to Jorge Miota the first use of the word in print—again, with an *h* in place of the *g*—and credit him with being the first to name and analyze this peculiarly Peruvian kind of flamboyance.

Huachafería is a complex phenomenon, and to dismiss or disregard it is to fail to understand this country and the psychology and the culture of many, perhaps most, of Peru's people. *Huachafería* is a vision of the world as well as an aesthetics: a way of feeling, thinking, and rejoicing, a mode of self-expression and a criterion for judgment.

We may relate it to kitsch, which has often been described as a distortion of taste. A person is kitsch when he imitates something—refinement or elegance—and falls short. His endeavor is a cheap caricature of his aesthetic model. Here is where *huachafería* differs. *Huachafería* has no model. It is not the deformation of a model, but the proposal of one; rather than perverting refinement and elegance, it gives them a specific and uniquely Peruvian form.

Any definition of *huachafería* is like chain mail: it may seem solid when seen from a distance, but it will allow essential elements of this diffuse, hard-to-define concept to slip through its innumerable gaps. For this reason, it is advisable to choose a few examples that give some idea of its character and breadth.

There is an aristocratic *huachafería* and a proletarian *huachafería*, but the middle classes are where it reigns most forcefully. It can be found everywhere, at least in the cities. In the countryside, it doesn't exist. If you find it in a campesino, he must have lived for a long time in town. *Huachafería* is irrational and sentimental: it sees the world through the lens of emotion and sensation long before reason appears; from the perspective of *huachafería*, ideas are dispensable, merely decorative, and often an obstacle to the free flow of feelings. The creole vals is the purest musical expression of *huachafería*, so much so that it is possible to affirm that no good vals is without it. All the greatest composers were aware of this, and it explains the nature of their lyrics, which are often impenetrable to ordinary interpretation but burst with fiery color, iridescent passion, erotic malice, and formidable rhetorical excesses that mark the starkest contrast with the relative absence of ideas.

Huachafería can be brilliant, but it is rarely intelligent: it is intuitive, verbose, solemn, melodic, imaginative, and, above all, maudlin. Whoever is immune to it will struggle to understand and appreciate the creole vals, unlike the *huaino*, a music from the mountains that rarely partakes of *huachafería* and, when it does, often misses the mark.

There is a contrast between *huachafería* in the cities of the mountains and that of the coast. Indigenism—the sentimental, literary, political, and historical employment of a romantic Peru before the arrival of the Spaniards—is the trademark of the *huachafería* of the hill country; it is evident, above all, in Puno and Cuzco, but it can be found throughout the Sierra. Hispanism, on the other hand, tends toward an idealization of colonial Peru. These two schools have their standard-bearers in two historians: Luis E. Valcárcel and José de la Riva Agüero, respectively. A middle point between them, a sui generis figure, is José Uriel García, author of *The New Indian*. He describes the Andes themselves as a living being, a presence that transformed the Spanish invaders in such a way that Spanish and Indian were indissolubly mingled, making the Spaniard Peruvian and the Indian Spanish, to a greater or lesser degree.

Inti Raymi, a celebration that takes place every year in Cuzco with thousands attending, is the height of *huachafería* every bit as much as the procession of Our Lord of Miracles that empurples (and this verb, too, is *huachafería*) Lima every year in October.

Huachafería is, by its nature, more closely related to certain doings than others, but there is no occupation or activity that excludes it outright. A speech, if it is to seduce the nation, must include a dash of *huachafería*. A politician who fails to gesticulate, who gets to the point instead of talking in circles, who avoids metaphors and talks drily instead of singing and growling, will struggle to reach the hearts of his listeners. When we speak of a "great orator" in Peru—take Víctor Raúl Haya de la Torre, the socialist founder of *aprismo*—we are speaking of someone florid and flamboyant, theatrical, operatic. In other words, a snake charmer.

Religion bears an intimate relation to *huachafería*. The

exact and natural sciences are deeply wary of it. The so-called social sciences—even this term already smacks of *huachafería*—feel an irresistible temptation toward it, and one is justified in asking whether it's even possible to call oneself a "social scientist" or a "political scientist" without engaging, in some way, in *huachafería*. Perhaps one can, but if so—if these men of social science are really so scientific—then I have the feeling of being slightly bamboozled, as when the bullfighter steps in the ring but lacks the courage to rile the bull.

Nowhere, perhaps, can the endless varieties of *huachafería* be better appreciated than in literature, because writing and speaking are its natural medium. There are poets who exhibit this quality sporadically, like César Vallejo, and others whose every verse reveals it, like José Santos Chocano. As a poet, Martín Adán was quite sober, but his prose was rife with *huachafería*. Julio Ramón Ribeyro is an odd case, a writer devoid of *huachafería*; in Peru, he is naturally the exception. More common are those like Alfredo Bryce Echenique and Salazar Bondy, who, despite their apparent prejudices against and phobia of *huachafería*, reveal it, like a badly hidden vice, in every line they compose. And then there's Manuel Scorza, whose very periods and commas positively drip with *huachafería*.

Allow me a brief list of notable examples of *huachafería*. In high society: dueling, bullfighting, owning a home in Miami, the use of nobiliary particles in your surname, anglicisms, and, of course, calling yourself white. In the middle classes: watching telenovelas and acting them out in real life, taking stockpots of noodles to the beach on Sundays to gobble them up between breaking waves, saying "I think" when you're not thinking at all, using diminutives (a *nip* of champagne), stressing your own or someone else's Indian heritage, for better or for worse, when convenience strikes. For the workers: wearing pomade, chewing gum, smoking marijuana, dancing to rock and roll, and being racist.

The surrealists said that the archetypal surrealist act was to walk outside and shoot the first person you saw on the street. The emblematic act of *huachafería* is that of the boxer with a battered face calling out to his mother, who is watching him on TV and praying for his victory, or maybe of the failed suicide who opens his eyes and asks for a priest to take his confession.

Huachafería has a tender side (the girl who buys red panties with lace to turn her boyfriend on). It may crop up in the strangest places—in the words and deeds of Marxist priests, for example. *Huachafería* gives a perspective from which to observe and organize the world and society. Argentina and India, if we judge from their films, are closer to it than, say, Finland. The Greeks had it, the Spartans didn't. Among religions, Catholicism naturally takes the gold here. In painting, *huachafería* is most evident in Rubens; among centuries, it's strongest in the eighteenth; regarding monuments, there's a tie between Sacré Coeur in Paris and the Valley of the Fallen in Spain. There are entire historical eras that seem based on a foundation of *huachafería*: the Byzantine Empire, the reign of Ludwig II of Bavaria, the Restoration. There are words that do little more than announce *huachafería*'s presence: "pristine," "societal," "sensitize," "honey" (spoken to a grown man or woman), "openness," "mindful," "afterglow."

The Venezuelans have a similar term, *pava*, that comes close to *huachafería*. I remember reading examples of it in

Salvador Garmendia: a naked woman shooting pool, a curtain of tears, wax flowers, a fishbowl in the living room. But for the Venezuelans, *pava* connotes bad fortune or foretells disaster. Its Peruvian counterpart is thankfully free of such overtones.

I should add here that I have written these lines without arrogance, with no desire to ridicule my subject, but rather warmly and sincerely, filled with wonder at that marvelous creation of God that is my brother: mankind itself!

XXVII

"So, you published your book, compadre. And Lala and I never even found out," Toni Lagarde complained.

"I didn't tell you about the presentation because I didn't want you to have to go all the way to the Ministry of Education," Toño replied. "I thought it better to come here myself to give you a copy. We'll see what you think of it."

The two friends were strolling down the Avenida Arica, slowly, because Toni walked with a cane. They were nearing the monument to Colonel Francisco Bolognesi, the Avenida Brasil, and the hordes of buses and cars. It was getting warmer, and the sidewalk was full of passersby.

"Lala and I will have to fight to see who reads it first," Toni said.

Toni tapped the ground with his cane as he walked with slow, long strides, stepping aside at times to let a group of people pass. He was dressed simply in thin trousers and a short-sleeved shirt frayed from many washings. He tried to avoid the potholes the avenue was dotted with as they passed the low, nondescript buildings with their big windows. Toño described to him his visit to the Palermo, where he sat next to two men talking about his book, and that remark the older one had made, about how the author must have lost his marbles. Toño had a feeling there, amid the multitude, that all of them were members of a great family; to make this known, he told Toni, would be his personal contribution to the history of Peru. He was leaving behind a guidebook, he said: a vision of creole music as the key to defeating prejudice and opening hearts and minds. If it had brought Toni and Lala together, why couldn't it do the same for the rest of Peru? It might sound mad, but it wasn't just some spur-of-the-moment notion. Toño had spent his entire life thinking about this, and he was sure that once his book became better known, the calls would come in for music education in the schools, so that children would begin, as soon as possible, to learn about their connection to the nation's traditions. They would be taught to play instruments, to sing the classics, and there would be dance classes teaching the marinera, the vals, and the polka. Differences would be reconciled, the gaps between the classes closed, rich whites like Toni would find happiness with poor blacks like Lala, and wealthy white women would fall into the arms of black, Indian, and mestizo men, poor men like Toño himself.

Toni listened in silence, took the book from under his arm and paged through it, tried to find confirmation of the hypotheses Toño kept mentioning. He hadn't wanted to say anything, but Toño kept asking insistently, "Am I right? Don't you think I'm right?" It seemed evident to him now, when the Shining Path had been defeated, that the solution to the country's problems was to awaken a new kind of patriotism as expressed in the vals and in creole music in general.

"I don't know, Toño," Toni said. "What happened with Lala and me, that was exceptional. Love, you know, it's a mystery. Always. I can't say we're an example of anything. We lived the life we wanted to. Maybe other people do the same."

"Other people are slaves to prejudice," Toño protested. "You're the only ones who are free. And music opened your eyes. It made you two aware."

"I'm not saying you're wrong," Toni replied, trying to calm his friend down. "You've got a theory there, but there are lots of theories. Like the *apristas*, remember how they thought it was the middle class that would unify Peru. And all of South America. But then the military stepped in and Haya de la Torre never managed to make it happen."

Toño reached behind his back, contorting his body and scratching compulsively. The Avenida Arica seemed to him suddenly hostile, full of crannies and crevices where rats and mice could hide out and breed. There must be thousands of them. He turned to Toni and proposed they return to his place. "I wouldn't mind a bit of your wife's quince preserves."

Toni smiled. "As soon as we heard you were coming, Lala went out to find quinces. They're not easy to get at this time of year. She managed, though. She only ever makes the stuff when she knows you're coming by."

"You two are amazing," Toño said. "Say what you want, but you deserve a book. Mine may not be about you exactly, but you're there, on almost every page. You're an example to everyone in Peru."

They walked a bit faster on their return, hoping to make it to Toni and Lala's home before the sun had set.

"Do you think I'm losing my marbles, to quote the man

who was talking about me at the Palermo?" Toño asked, impatient, scratching his legs.

"Why would you ask that, Toño? You're not crazy, you're an idealist, and there's nothing wrong with that."

When they arrived, Lala had already laid out the tea for them in their small dining room, remembering that Toño always took his with a few drops of milk, and the buns were warm on their plates, with a generous slathering of marmalade.

"Toño's brought us his book," Toni told his wife. "You won't believe how nice the dedication is. According to him, you and I are an example for all Peruvians to follow."

"See, Toni? That's what I've always told you," Lala responded jokingly. "We're exceptional; it's just that you never believe me."

"I mean it seriously," Toño interjected with a solemn tone. "You two are a model, the way you've lived. Just being happy instead of always searching for happiness. There are few people like that, here or anywhere else. I guess it sounds silly when I put it that way. But I've never met another couple like you, and I wish everyone in Peru would take a page out of your book. It's not just your marriage, though that was something—standing up to the absurd prejudices and ideas about class we have in this country—it's also the way you've endured, the way you've been happy with what you have, not asking for more. I repeat, you're an example to the whole of Peru."

"What about you and Matilde?" Lala asked. "You're a better couple than we are. Toni gets on my nerves more than you know."

Toño looked down, settled back in his chair. It was kind of her to pretend for his sake, but it wasn't true. "Trust me," he said, "it's not the same."

It wasn't the same because an abyss had opened up between him and Matilde, one that was inevitable when two people couldn't enjoy the good things in life. They didn't dance, didn't listen to music together, they devoted their hours to the struggle to survive. And Toño took advantage of Matilde. He knew that. She wore her fingers to the bone washing and sewing while he sat around fantasizing about Cecilia Barraza. If anything, creole music had come between him and his wife. The more Toño worked away on his book, passing endless hours in the National Library, the more time Matilde had to devote to their household, to keeping their daughters and even him afloat. She broke her back while he chased a ghost: the fantasy that his book would raise him to Cecilia's level, that his prestige would overcome that resistance that kept her from seeing him as a real man, someone to sleep with, someone to accompany her on life's path.

A cloud settled over Toño's brow, and he no longer seemed to enjoy his snack as he said somberly, "The funny thing is, I don't even think you two realize you're happy."

He might have added that, unlike him and Matilde, Toni and Lala had relied on their love to get them through every hardship: prejudice, poverty, the ups and downs of a life that had been far from easy. Their love had never waned, and it had been their shield, their secret. He saw this in what remained of the afternoon, as their conversation turned to current events in Peru. They talked about the terrorist attacks, the poverty in the mountains, the news, and Toño noticed that even if Toni and Lala were upset or alarmed, their closeness defended them against any blows life might deal, any bad turn fate might take. That was serendipity. You couldn't just tell people, "I command you to love each other forever," you couldn't pass a law that they had to be like Toni and Lala. Love being transitory, that was the normal thing: you meet different people, you fall in love again, you go from person to person. The exception was for love to remain and grow stronger. Toño had wanted that with Matilde, but it hadn't been possible, and this made him question the central thesis of his book. Maybe he should have been a bit more hesitant, a little less optimistic. He was taciturn as he said his goodbyes to Toni and Lala.

When he got home, he was told he'd received an urgent call from Cabada, his publisher. He walked to Collau's bar and called him back. Cabada was frantic. He'd been trying to get ahold of Toño for days, he'd been leaving messages at the bar, he supposed those damn little girls either hadn't written them down or had failed to pass them along.

"What is it, then?" Toño asked. "Is everything all right?"

"I'd say so. Your book's sold two thousand copies. That's the entire print run. And booksellers are writing me asking for more. We'll need a second edition. It seems they've flown off the shelves."

Toño listened with relish to the old bookseller's enthusiastic words. He was shocked at first, and didn't know what to say. But then he managed to get out a proviso: "I should take this opportunity to correct a few things, Mr. Cabada. There are quite a few errors in the first edition, and a few ideas I should probably examine a little more closely."

"Forget that for now," Cabada said. "You go ahead and

make your notes and whatnot, but for the future. The second edition needs to come out now. We've got to strike while the iron is hot. I have orders coming in from all over the provinces. You and I should meet. As soon as possible. I've gone ahead and drafted a new contract I need you to sign. It'll bring a bit of coin your way. I'll see you at ten tomorrow morning at your favorite place, the Bransa. Sound good? Oh, and let me congratulate you. Even I didn't imagine your book would sell this well."

He hung up, and Toño felt the rats crawling all over his body. So this was it. The news stirred and terrified him. Two thousand copies sold. Was it really possible? Toño wanted to tell Cecilia Barraza, but that would mean writing her a letter and meeting with her two or three days later, and he needed to clear his head now, even if it was to Collau or Matilde. His friend would bring out a bottle for him; the occasion would be festive. Cecilia, though . . . Yes, he would write her. He would ask her to meet him on Thursday. Or better yet, Friday. With the weekend ahead of her, she'd likely be less pressed for time.

XXVIII

There was a time when more than fifteen hundred languages and dialects were spoken in Latin America. Some linguists claim that this is an exaggeration, that the number is closer to a thousand; others have claimed there were five thousand, perhaps more. Regardless, what is evident is that the early Americans didn't understand each other, and this explains the abundance of bloody wars across the continent. Latin America, as the first Spanish conquistadors found it, was an orgy of bloodshed, a continent marked by a thousand battles.

Spanish spread like a mist across this sea of languages and dialects, integrating the different peoples, and from then on—apart from the military campaigns and dictatorships of the nineteenth century, which were violent and, without exception, disastrous for our countries' development—the peoples of these different lands ceased to kill each other and learned to live together more or less pacifically.

This unification through language was the best thing that could have happened to Latin America. Spanish unites us from Mexico to Argentina, and even in Brazil, more and more people are speaking Spanish all the time. The language continues to range across the globe without the aid of any government or state, thanks to its virtues, its simplicity, its clear structures, the ease with which it's spoken; and with emigration, Spanish is now the tongue of hundreds of millions across the globe.

Mexico has the largest number of Spanish speakers, followed by the United States, where more than sixty million speak it to a greater or lesser degree. There is debate here, however: some say that Spanish speakers who reside in the United States eventually lose their language, with English replacing it. The evidence isn't clear. I've heard that there are families where Spanish stubbornly abides across the generations the way muscle clings to bone.

So let us give the conquistadors this one thing: where else in the world can you travel from one extreme of a continent to another, understanding everything the people say and being understood by everyone? Can you do that in Africa, in Asia? In Europe, it's a known fact that you either learn languages or you're condemned to silence when you leave your home country.

There are some who justify the conquest in terms not of language, but of religion. They will recall how, thanks to Father Bartolomé de las Casas and others like him, Spain permitted a debate at the University of Salamanca on the question of whether Indians possessed souls or whether they were, instead, like the animals of the forest. De las Casas's extraordinary oratorical skills resolved the question: to a man, the prelates agreed that the Indians did have souls and therefore deserved protection and instruction in the true faith.

The reader will wonder whether the author of these pages is Catholic himself. I must respond with a confession. Despite those hard days when I think of death and of the rats that will come to devour my body, days when dread overtakes me and I pray and feel in myself the truth of the religion the brothers at the Colegio La Salle inculcated in me, I've often told myself that the Bible was written for the uncultured, and that no educated person can accept it blindly. Am I a believer? Sometimes yes and sometimes no. I have believed in Christ, in the Virgin Mary, in the Passion and the Resurrection, but I also have great doubts. And I question the way the Catholic Church has spread across the globe, bringing with it sanctimoniousness and prohibitions. Didn't Gonzalo Toledo say, in *Let Me Tell You*, that the Catholic Church nearly forbade the vals because the man touched the woman's back while dancing?

And yet it is a fact that human beings live better with religion than without it. Christianity gives order to barbaric disunities, and it is a common denominator for Latin America's peoples, in other respects so different. And so, to the question of whether it is better that Christianity exist, I must answer in the affirmative, so long as it keeps its hands off of creole music. We need freedom, mischief, mirth, we need that hand placed on the back. There are times when my superstitions from my schoolboy days at La Salle come back to haunt me, but deep down, I'm an atheist. I have many doubts about the existence of purgatory and hell, and I struggle to believe that God would condemn anyone to eternal flames or tortures meted out by demons for something as silly as skipping Mass. These are medieval notions that don't stand up to modern scrutiny.

As for the soul, whatever it is, whether or not it exists, I cannot accept the fact that it, and the human beings who house it, and everything else will disappear, that we are fated to become a mound of bones. And yet the thought of the soul outliving the body is a little difficult for me to swallow. My father, like a good Italian, was a believer, and the things he and the priests taught me at school on the Avenida Arica ring true to me at some times, but at others they fall short.

Am I saying that the Spanish language and the Catholic religion suffice to justify the conquest of Latin America? No. It's not that easy, my friends. If the English had conquered Latin America, they'd have slaughtered the natives the way they did in the United States, and the indigenous population would number no more than the Apaches and their like in the North America of today. Spain built churches, universities, printing presses, courts in the conquered territories; from the beginning, it perceived Latin America as significant, Spain's double on the other side of the Atlantic. The Spanish founded viceroyalties and captaincies here, but of course, they also brought over the Inquisition with the same fanatical torturers who spread suffering in the metropole.

The Spanish landowners were wicked and exploitative, but the Spanish crown and its representatives tried to mitigate their excesses and their crimes against the Indians. As a result, the landowners rose up and challenged the Spanish monarchy. Horrible wars were a consequence. This happened in Peru, and the laws targeting the Indians grew crueler, as did their consequences, so that the natives died off like flies. Even today, they remain a disadvantaged class that must be granted the power and status it deserves.

XXIX

Toño Azpilcueta slipped into the Bransa and took his usual table, the one where he sat upon leaving the library. He was wearing the same jacket and tie he had worn to his book presentation at the Ministry of Education. Looking back, he wished he had invited Cecilia Barraza to it. Had she heard him speaking so clearly and enthusiastically about his book, perhaps in the depths of her mind a spark would have flared up, the possibility that he could be more than a friend. To Cecilia, he was just a scribbler, his columns, full of passing news about the world of creole music, published in magazines that had little to no impact on the wider public. But now, Toño thought, he was an author whose book had sold out its first edition and was being discussed in Lima's finest cafés. Didn't that change things? The man Cecilia was coming to meet was no longer a nobody secretly striving to join the intellectual elite, but instead a writer who was changing Peru's entire conception of itself. Was that overstating things? He doubted it. He was confident that his ideas would be discussed in the universities, the press, the coffee shops, the social clubs, and that he would soon achieve a fame comparable to that of the musicians who were his subject.

When he saw Cecilia walk into the Bransa and spot

him, he stood, smoothed his suit jacket, and waved at her sheepishly.

"What was the rush, Toño? Couldn't you have given me a bit more notice if you needed me?" she asked, kissing him on the cheek and sitting down.

"Nice to see you, too, my beautiful Cecilia, stranger to all that is ugly in humanity," he said with a smile.

"Now that's *huachafería*," she told him with a laugh. "I'm assuming you've got good news since you're all dressed up and speaking in poetry."

"The first edition of my book sold out, and the publisher's bringing out a second one," Toño responded. "I wanted to tell you in person."

Cecilia saw the gleam in his eye and noticed the strange tone in his voice. Even his smile had something odd about it.

"You look very pleased," she said, "and I'm happy for you. I just hope it won't go to your head."

"I am and will always be the same man," Toño affirmed, reaching across the table to stroke Cecilia's hand. "Especially if you tell me not to change."

"To tell the truth, I'd say you've changed already," Cecilia told him, pulling her hand away and hiding it under the table. "Don't forget, Toño, you and I are just friends."

"Let's drop the hypocrisy. That was before. I'm a real intellectual now. It's time for me to aim higher."

Toño stood and bent over quickly, trying to kiss Cecilia Barraza on the lips. Her eyes opened wide as she pulled away. Before she could stop herself, she reached up and slapped Toño on the cheek. It wasn't loud or hard, just a dry clap, and no one noticed apart from the guests at the table next to them. Feeling his face flush, Toño turned to look at them. The burning sensation crept down his neck, where it became an itch, into his arms and torso, and finally down to his legs, and then he saw them everywhere, big and fat, cross-eyed, their pointy snouts, their exposed teeth. They were under the tables, between them, one leapt from Cecilia's head into an empty chair next to her. Unable to hold back, he began scratching himself all over. He pushed up the sleeves of his jacket, opened the collar of his shirt, tried frantically to rid himself of those nasty creatures that were surrounding him and crawling up his pants.

Cecilia observed him, disconcerted, baffled as to what was going on. Even the rest of the customers were perplexed and unsettled at this man scratching and slapping himself and kicking like Héctor Chumpitaz, the legendary soccer player.

"Toño, what's wrong with you? Calm down, please!" Cecilia demanded.

"You don't see them, do you?" Toño asked. "They're everywhere. I know you can't see them, no one does, but trust me, they're there."

Cecilia, realizing that something was very wrong with Toño, knew she needed to act quickly, before he alarmed the other customers and the situation got out of control. She swiftly took Toño's arm and dragged him out beneath the dark wood balconies onto the Plaza de Armas. There, she forced him to sit on a bench surrounded by tall palm trees in the middle of the square, and asked him to tell her what was going on.

Toño continued scratching himself, contorting his face, opening and closing his eyes, but he was now somewhat less desperate.

"This has been happening to me since I was a boy," he said. "Whenever I get agitated. It feels like I'm covered in rats. They gnaw at my back, and I get this urge to take off my shirt and pants and scratch myself until I draw blood. I've never told anyone. You're the first. And I don't know what to do about it, Cecilia. I'm at the end of my rope. I know the rats don't exist. I know I've invented them. I've been doing it for as long as I can remember. And the itching . . . it's driving me insane. I can't bear it anymore."

Cecilia told him not to worry, she would help him. She flagged down a taxi and instructed the driver to take them to the San Isidro district. Toño went on scratching his legs and back and, when he couldn't reach the center of his back, rubbed himself up and down against the seat, finding some slight relief. What seemed like an eternity passed, and the taxi stopped at last. Cecilia paid, took Toño's arm, and dragged him toward a new-looking building.

They found themselves in the offices of Doctor Quispe, which looked out onto an expanse of gardens that were empty at that hour. In the middle was a fountain with water jetting into the air. A nurse guided them to a waiting area and remained there with Toño while Cecilia entered the doctor's office to speak with him. Toño could see him in his freshly ironed white lab coat. He kissed Cecilia on the cheek with a confidence that hinted at long and perhaps intimate acquaintance, then closed the door. A few minutes later, he called Toño in and invited him to sit in a thick, comfortable armchair. Bending over him with a serious mien, he said, "Well, my friend. Let's hear about that itching that's tormenting you, those little rats you've been inventing since you were a boy."

Stammering, feeling ridiculous and on the verge of

despair, Toño spoke. Cecilia watched the two men from a prudent distance. She appeared nervous. After hearing Toño's story, Doctor Quispe paced briefly, called for his nurse, said something to her, and sent her away. A few seconds later, she returned with some pills and a glass of clear water.

"Take this. It'll get rid of that dreadful itching. Here, follow me."

He guided Toño and Cecilia to the room next door, motioning for them to sit down in some very new, luxurious armchairs made of gleaming wood, with green cushions printed with Egyptian figures. He sat down across from them.

"You have," he said, "what we call an obsession. When you were a child, you must have associated rats with some negative feeling. Maybe it was the fear of failure, or of abandonment, or of strangers. Of something, at any rate. Rejection, perhaps. We'll figure it out later. What we can be sure of is that it's the origin of this physical discomfort, which I have no doubt comes to plague you in your most difficult moments. Trust me, your case is far from exceptional. I would even say it's quite common here in Lima. Do you feel better? Don't worry about the pills, they were just a little something to calm you down."

The doctor grimaced slightly, and Toño nodded like a chastised child, unable to look him in the eyes. He wished he'd never dared to throw himself at Cecilia.

"These sorts of manias are very widespread, not just here, but all over the world. You find them in men and women, in old people and children. But with a bit of persistence and a little therapy, I can assure you we'll cure yours. Relax, my friend. The situation is far from hopeless."

"I'll pay, Doctor," Cecilia said. "Toño and I are old friends. And besides, I'm the one who brought him here."

"I should offer you a finder's fee for all the patients you send my way, Cecilia. You've kept starvation at bay for me," Doctor Quispe said. He was an elegant man with silver hair and perfect teeth—a gentleman. He smiled easily, but despite his friendly appearance, there was something penetrating in his gaze that unsettled Toño. Perhaps it was just his own shame, though. What a spectacle he'd put on, scratching himself all over like a maniac! Now that the itch had abated, he felt a bit lightheaded and drowsy. He covered his mouth for a long yawn.

"If you like," the doctor said, "you can rest a moment in the waiting room while Cecilia and I are talking. The medicine may have made you drowsy—that's fairly common."

Without a word, Toño slunk out, head hanging, resigned to letting the doctor flirt with Cecilia behind his back. His guilt at making a scene was getting worse by the second. He closed his eyes and lay back in a chair, and when he opened them again—he assumed he'd dozed for a few minutes—Cecilia and Doctor Quispe were standing at the door, taking leave of each other, apparently. Toño stood as well.

The doctor glanced at his watch and asked Toño if he was feeling better.

"Much better, Doctor. I can't tell you how much I hate bothering you like this."

"It's nothing," Quispe said. "Cecilia and I have worked out the details in the meantime. Can you come in on Thursday evenings, around seven? If so, we'll get to exterminating these rats you've invented."

In that moment, Toño wished he could disappear. The

thought of Cecilia paying for his therapy . . . he couldn't imagine anything more embarrassing! But he certainly couldn't offer to do it himself. He had just enough in his pocket to pay for their breakfast. And to judge by the doctor's debonair appearance, a session with him wasn't cheap.

Still, he managed to get out the words: "Thank you, Doctor. Thank you very much. Thursday, is it? Understood, yes, I'll be here."

"Perfect," Quispe said, shaking his hand. Again, he kissed Cecilia on the cheek. Then he opened the door for them and told them goodbye.

"I can't tell you how embarrassed I am, Cecilia," Toño confessed as they waited for the elevator. "You paid for the taxi, you paid for the appointment. I'm frightened to ask how much I owe you."

"You owe me nothing, Toño. What are friends for if not moments like this? Don't worry about it."

"Friends . . ." he repeated, watching the numbers light up on the elevator display. "Listen, what I said earlier at the Bransa . . ."

"Don't worry about it. I've seen you in these moments of *huachafería* before." She laughed. "You get sentimental, I understand. There's nothing wrong with it. And now we've cleared everything up."

They walked outside, and Cecilia smiled deliciously, looking slightly rushed as she waved to him and got into the first taxi that passed. Toño stood there alone on the sidewalk, trying to memorize the address of Doctor Quispe's office. He would go back there the following week, not because he wanted to, but because he had to. This obsession with rats needed to end. As did his obsession with Cecilia Barraza.

XXX

Patient reader, allow me another of my confessions: I don't hold Tahuantinsuyo, the Inca Empire, in especially high esteem. I feel some pride in its existence, in the dominion it exercised in its short life—a hundred years, more or less—over Ecuador and Bolivia, parts of Chile and Colombia, and even the border regions of Argentina and Brazil. But there is something in this past that sits ill with me: the system the emperors in Cuzco devised for dealing with the wayward and unruly, those who murmured their objections to the empire's institutions and might later on have shown allegiance to dissident leaders. The system in question was known as *mitma*, which could be translated from Quechua as "expatriation" or "exile," and the exiles themselves are called *mitimaes*. These lesser dissidents were ejected from Cuzco and confined to distant towns and regions. Naturally, they felt alienated there: often they didn't speak the local language, and they had to live and work surrounded by people who disdained them, knowing that their punishment would have no end, that they would be buried there in the midst of strangers. Historians and anthropologists learned of the *mitimaes* centuries later, when they discovered in Ancash and Ayacucho, places far from Cuzco, populations that spoke the Quechua of Cuzco and the midlands, very different from the local variety: these people, researchers recognized, were the descendants of dissidents exiled from Tahuantinsuyo.

I feel a strange kind of solidarity with those hundreds or even thousands of men and women torn from their habitat and forced by the reigning powers to scrape by through their own means. I imagine the sorrow and melancholy those men and women must have felt; I chafe at the unfairness of labeling them dissidents; I imagine their feeling of helplessness upon arriving in those strange, often hostile lands many miles from their homes. What would a person from Cuzco do when confined to Ancash, Tumbes, or Cajamarca? I imagine the loneliness of exile for them was in some ways comparable to the existential condition of Lalo Molfino, left in a trash heap in Puerto Etén as fodder for insects and rats. Peru's sorrow, that wistfulness that is characteristic of almost all of us, may have its seeds in the experience of exile from the old imperial regime, in those groups of migrants forced to live on memories alone.

The commonplace—accepted by most historians—is that the Incans were illiterate. But certain Spanish chroniclers cast doubt on this conclusion, and I think it more likely that we lack evidence of literacy because the Incan nobles refused to teach their vassals to read, realizing, as have many oppressors across time, that writing and books are subversive, and inevitably harmful to those in power. This was as true in the sixteenth century as it is now. The closest equivalent of writing that we know of is a system of knotted strings used for quantitative recordkeeping. Piles of these were found in the administrative buildings, palaces, and other Inca structures in Cuzco and the main provinces of the empire. Dozens of specialists inside and outside of Peru have spent their lives trying to decipher this so-called writing, which is not an alphabet per se, but rather a mnemonic pattern for memorizing large numbers, as was necessary for the infinite functionaries in the immense bureaucracy of the Inca Empire.

This accounting system is prototypical of the carefully preserved vertical structure that allowed the Incan dictatorship to continue as long as it did. But in the end, these efforts were in vain, because rivalry flared up between Cuzco and Quito, and by the time the conquistadors arrived, Tahuantinsuyo was split between the enemy brothers Atahualpa and Huáscar, whose armies fought each other ferociously for control of each other's territories. When the first Spaniards arrived in Cuzco, they reported seeing long lines of crucified bodies left there by soldiers from Quito after laying siege to the empire's capital.

Pizarro conducted himself poorly with Atahualpa. After capturing him, the Spaniard promised him freedom if his subjects would fill one room of the temple of Cajamarca with gold and another two with silver. Atahualpa kept his word and filled the rooms, but Pizarro broke his promise and had Atahualpa killed. Then again, virtually all the leading conquistadors died violently as a final consequence of their obsessive greed, even Pizarro, who was stabbed to death by his countrymen. Columbus himself was reviled for his excessive love for precious stones, things that for the Incas had no monetary value and served only to pay homage to their gods. How could they understand the thirst for gold of those bearded men who betrayed each other daily in order to lay their hands on such riches?

The three centuries of colonial rule that followed don't strike me as all too inspiring, either; this is my last confession before leaving the reader in peace. That country full of churches and convents, processions and Masses, with the Spanish using all their energies to spread the Catholic faith, turning the natives and themselves into fanatics, is not something one can easily admire. The believers' lives—the lives of all Peruvians in those days—strike me as a kind of living death. There were, of course, figures among them worthy of our respect, cultured people who managed to lift their heads above that perverse, mutilated culture—Pedro Peralta y Barnuevo comes to mind—but such erudition, tainted as it was by pietism, was characteristic of a tiny minority, while the masses were mired in ignorance and confusion, which would abide until the advent of the creole vals and other types of local music that would make Peru a truly diverse country with that particular sensibility we can be proud of.

Did Lalo Molfino dream of such a thing? He can't have been a learned man, and knew too little of anything beyond music to ever devote much thought to it. But intuitively, with that sixth sense true creators have, those demiurges whose works give entire eras their character, I am certain that he glimpsed this ideal, this vision of what his country would and should become.

Might creole music have the power to change the course of history? To make Peru a great country as it was in the past, a font of riches and ideas, of stories and music that can cross land and sea to be read, sung, and danced to by men and women across the globe? Why not? Tango managed it, with Gardel and all those other musicians who are now so famous. If Peru could move past its psychology of pure survival, if it became a prosperous nation thanks to its music, perhaps its place in the world would change as well, and it would work its way into that group of countries where things are decided—war and peace, tragedy and glory—for the sake of the people's happiness. Surely I won't live to see it, but I am certain that the life and work of Lalo Molfino and the ideas I have set down here will contribute to it becoming true. Like Mariátegui's *Seven Interpretive Essays on Peruvian Reality*, the poetry of César Vallejo, or the writings of Ricardo Palma, this book you hold in your hands, reader, will be the starting point of a true revolution that will pull our Peru up from poverty and sorrow, restoring its glory and its creativity, making it a place where all are truly equal, and putting an end to the sad divisions of its people.

XXXI

The following Monday, Toño awoke early, just as the sun was rising. He washed and dressed, and when he arrived at the Bransa, he opened the door, imagining he would see Antenor Cabada. But his publisher had yet to arrive. Toño sat down at his table and ordered a chamomile tea, taking little sips of it as he waited. His stomach no longer bothered him, his legs and back no longer itched. Doctor Quispe's pills had done him good. If only he'd asked for a prescription.

Antenor arrived soon afterward, shook his hand, and announced, "Here's the contract for you to sign, Toño. And a few *soles* as an advance payment—I assume you can use them. That second edition is taking too long, though."

"I need a few more days to correct the text, Antenor. And you can keep your money," Toño replied. This was the first time they'd addressed each other in such familiar terms.

Toño wanted to revise parts of the book to refute the remarks he'd overheard in the Café Palermo, to anticipate other possible criticisms, and to reinforce his ideas.

"We need to strike while the iron's hot, Toño," Cabada said.

Cabada was an older man, dressed simply in a summer shirt that couldn't have been warm enough on that chilly day. He had no wife or children that Toño knew of. He had a bachelor's look about him. He was well shaved, and the expression behind his glasses was anxious.

"What do a few more days matter?" Toño asked firmly, uninclined to give in to his publisher's demands.

"Toño, you may think otherwise, but the situation you're in isn't something that happens often," Cabada said, nose twitching, hands waving about. "The book's in demand, and even once I have the manuscript in hand, it will take weeks to get printed copies out to the provinces. A book has a brief life, and it's soon forgotten—we've got to sell while we can. You don't know how lucky you are. Even without promotion, your book is getting around. You can make your corrections afterward, and we'll put them in the third edition. Because there will be a third edition, I can tell you that right now, Toño. If you want, I'll put it to paper. But the second one, we need it printed yesterday!"

Without irony, without modesty, Toño countered him: "I'm not looking to get rich. All I want is for my book to be good. For the ideas in it to be expressed properly. A week—give me a week, at least. I promise you that next Monday, you'll have the corrected manuscript. You can bring out a second edition that even the most demanding readers won't be able to find fault with."

By his face, Toño could tell Cabada wasn't happy. He had let his coffee get cold. He was weary of trying to convince Toño, who was glancing around at the customers now pouring into the Bransa, many of whom he recognized—solitary men, most of them, taking their breakfast before going to the office. There were no whites among them, no

Indians, either—only mixed-race middle-class workers with stiff hair, cut short or smoothed down with pomade.

"Fine, Toño, fine. I'll give you a week. But not a day more," the publisher said, his brow furrowed. "And don't forget, I need ten to fifteen days, sometimes longer, for the new edition to be delivered after I send the order to the printer. We'll hope they're not too busy right now. And then we've got to box the books up and ship them out to the provinces and to the shops here in Lima. It's a mistake wasting more time over a few little typos, Toño. But you've convinced me. A week. Don't make me regret this."

He ordered another coffee, strong, without milk, and a buttered bun. Toño was glum, feeling that he'd ruined his publisher's morning, but he was determined to correct his book: to polish certain of the ideas, to add more examples, perhaps to find some other issue essential to the question of Peruvian identity. More music, more songs—and religion, because faith was an important question in the country, too; and bullfighting, and sports, maybe, yes—Héctor Chumpitaz, the old glories. A week would suffice: he'd work day and night, adding and revising until everything fit.

He asked Cabada, "You always wanted to be a publisher, didn't you?"

The older man nodded. "Yes, always. The bookstore was a fair business, but for me, it was a stepping stone. Working from ten in the morning to ten at night behind the counter . . . imagine! I needed a long time to attain my independence, though. The bookseller's job in Lima is no cakewalk. It's costly, and of course the taxman is always around the corner with some pretext to ask for more money."

"You should look on the bright side, then. You achieved your goal. You put out your first book, and it's doing well."

"Don't try and turn this around on me," Cabada said. "It's your book, and the longer you dawdle, the more money we're leaving on the table. I don't think you realize what a miracle it is that it's sold so well with so little coverage in the papers."

"So little? I think you mean none," Toño corrected him. "As far as I know, there hasn't been a single review. All those intellectuals out there, and not one has bothered to shine a light on my book's virtues. If it's made it this far, even out in the provinces, I have to assume that it's thanks to intelligent readers and word of mouth."

"Why question it?" Cabada said. "But if you want me to stroke your vanity, I'll show you some of the letters we've gotten from booksellers in Trujillo, Cuzco, Arequipa . . . I think it's doing better in those places than here, actually. That idea of yours about bringing Peru together through creole music, I think it has more appeal out there. Tell me the truth, though: Do you really think a couple of *huainitos* and marineras can bring equality to this country? Make the white people marry the mestizos and all that?"

"Absolutely!" Toño replied.

"I thought you were trying to be provocative, just to see if the idea took off," Cabada responded. "Never in my wildest dreams would I have thought you actually believed such a thing. Think of all the division in this country, social, racial, and economic, the prejudices . . . You think creole music's going to just fix all that?"

"See? Your objections show why I absolutely have to work on my book again before the second edition comes out. I can use the time to clear up the doubts people like you have." Toño leaned across the table as he continued, "I know there are points that are missing, but don't worry. Give me a week and you'll have a book that clears all this up."

"Good, good," Cabada agreed, sitting back. "Then do as you will, add pages—it's your book and there's no one more interested than I am in seeing these improvements. But one request: don't bog down the message. Your thesis is a charming one, and I think that's what's drawn readers in. Avoid the temptation to tinker too much with it."

Toño stood up, telling Cabada that he had no time to waste. The two men shook hands, and Toño hurried to the Avenida Abancay, to the National Library, which would, until the following Monday, be his home, his lair, his fortress. Feeling perplexed, Cabada watched him march away, kicking at the air, as though knocking aside little creatures that had crossed his path.

XXXII

During the two weeks he needed to edit and expand his book, Toño didn't see Doctor Quispe. He even forgot about his appointments. Had it not been for the insistence of Antenor Cabada, who began pestering him as soon as his deadline had passed, he'd have forgotten about Quispe entirely. But the pressure from his publisher aggravated his nerves, and once again he felt that intense irritation climbing up his legs, spreading across his back, and driving him to the library bathroom, where he could undress and scratch himself until he bled. Then he remembered the miraculous pills the psychiatrist had given him and resolved to attend his next session.

The nurse shot him a hostile look when she greeted him before inviting him into the waiting room where he had nodded off the last time he was there. Two Thursdays he had missed. That was a serious breach of decorum. Toño didn't even manage to sit down before she told him the doctor was ready for him. Quispe neither stood nor greeted him. He simply pointed to the chair where his patients normally sat.

"I truly apologize for not coming before, Doctor. But I have to tell you, I feel much better. The pills you gave me were the perfect thing to put my mind in order." Toño pointed at his temple as he said this. "If you give me a prescription, you won't have to worry about me bothering you."

Doctor Quispe looked up at the ceiling, hands folded together on his desk, and remained silent for a few seconds before admonishing him calmly: "If you're back, that means something's wrong. Have you seen a rat or two creeping around? Had some itching, maybe?"

"I've never felt better, Doctor," Toño said with a fake smile. "I'd just like to have a pill or two in reserve, in case I suddenly need it."

Quispe seemed not to hear him, or at least not to care what he was saying.

"It's evident that stress, tension, and anxiety are what triggers these itching attacks, Toño. And your hallucinations. Frustration, too, I'd wager. Impotence, maybe."

"No, Doctor, you're not listening to me," Toño said, sitting up straight. "I'm not here because anything's wrong. I appreciate your interest, but the last thing I need right now is a shrink rooting around in my brain. The pills are more than enough. If I could just get a prescription . . ."

"Azpilcueta," the doctor murmured, interrupting him. "That's a Basque name, isn't it?"

"The name, yes. But my father was Italian."

"Basque, but Italian," the doctor repeated. "Explain to me then how an expert in creole music and Peruvian affairs happens to be the son of a foreigner."

"He wasn't a foreigner," Toño Azpilcueta protested. "He was Peruvian just like anyone else. He lived in Peru from the time he was a boy."

It had been ages since Toño had talked about his father,

and now, Doctor Quispe's unforeseen question brought him insistently into his mind. What was the name of that tiny mountain village in Italy he had come from? How had he ended up in Peru? Toño recalled his father talking about it, how he could still remember the place where he'd spent the early years of his childhood, before his parents had brought him over . . . was it in Sicily? Toño wasn't sure, or perhaps he'd never known. His father had been a severe man, devoted day and night to his work on the railroad in the mountains. He had married Toño's mother in Chumbivilcas. She was a mestiza woman, and she pampered her husband. On the few occasions when Toño and his father were together, he'd ask him, "How are things going at La Salle?" He knew a fair bit about the Lasallians, because they'd built a school near his birthplace in Italy.

Toño repeated this story to Quispe. "You're speaking of your father in the past tense," Quispe said. "I assume, then, he is deceased. What was your relationship with him like?"

Toño saw himself in front of his father's coffin. How he'd wished his mother had been there, the mother he'd lost fifteen or sixteen years before. How lonely he'd felt. More so than at any moment in his life. He wished he had gotten along better with the old man, that he'd asked him those questions that now must remain forever unanswered. Like how he'd met Toño's mother. She'd liked that he was Italian, Toño seemed to remember, and that he had a good character. Toño couldn't remember any jealousy or arguments, anything like that. His father wouldn't have cared much about his book's success—that kind of thing never impressed him unless it translated into money. Toño recalled how a train inspector his father had known had gotten a sudden and generous raise, thanks to his contacts. For weeks, he had talked about the man with a mix of envy and admiration. And he'd flown into a rage when Toño had begun his courses at San Marcos and had chosen, regrettably, to specialize in Peruvian folk culture, of all things. Toño had started going to bars and concert halls, sitting around and talking with those in the know and writing about the singers and musicians he heard on the radio. One night his father followed him to a bar in Abajo el Puente. He'd assumed he'd find his son stinking drunk and strumming a guitar, or worse, beating a cajon or stroking a jawbone. Instead, he saw him looking attentive, scrawling lines in a notebook. That didn't stop him from upbraiding Toño for wasting his time with bohemian nonsense sure to land him in the poorhouse. He couldn't stand that kind of *huachafería*.

"Well now," Toño said, standing up as if emerging from a trance. "I didn't come to talk about all that. My prescription, Doctor—let's get that out of the way, and I won't waste any more of your time."

"Did you do the same thing with your father?" Doctor Quispe asked, uncrossing his legs and leaning over his desk to examine Toño more closely. "Did you avoid him? Run away from him?"

"I'm not avoiding or running away from anything," Toño said in irritation, walking back and forth. "The problem is, I'm telling you what I want and you're not listening."

"Toño, sit down, please. I know you want the pills, and I'll give them to you. But first, I'd like to know a few things. Your mother . . . did she also avoid confrontations with your father?"

"What the hell does my mother have to do with all this?" Toño shouted.

He sat back down, the image of his mother now palpable in his mind. Though he was young when she died, he could remember her love of creole music and how she had passed it down to him. They used to listen to famous players on the radio together. Toño could still remember all their names. He would lie in her arms and she would whisper the lyrics to him, and in those moments, he felt himself part of something bigger, something that would protect him from his father's cold rages. It was as if she and he had melted into one.

"Might this obsession of yours, this phobia regarding rats, have something to do with some fear you felt as a child?" Quispe asked, his voice soft, his pronunciation clear and precise.

"Please forgive me for what I'm about to say, Doctor, I realize courtesy is in order here, but you're backing me into a corner, and I have to tell you: everything you're saying is grade-A horseshit," Toño said, turning red with rage.

"Don't take it like that, Toño, I'm simply doing my job."

"I didn't come here for you to try to climb inside my head and root through my memories," Toño shouted. "I didn't give you permission for that. I don't need it, and I don't like it."

"What you're experiencing right now is a normal psychological process, Mr. Azpilcueta. It's called denial."

"I don't care what it's called. Leave my head alone," Toño said, pointing at his right temple again. "I'm not going to sit here and expose myself and let you kill off everything that has made me the person I am and that has allowed me to write the book I've written. Now listen to me: I crossed the whole damn city for a few pills, and if you're not going to give them to me, I'm leaving. I don't care. And I won't say it's been a pleasure, because it hasn't been. You're presumptuous, you're arrogant, and for your information, you don't have a shot with Cecilia Barraza!"

Toño walked out of the office, slamming the door. Too impatient to wait for the elevator, he rushed down the stairs. Unwilling to stand around waiting for a minibus to take him back to Villa El Salvador, he began to walk, telling himself he would simply keep going until weariness overcame him. Only then would he try to figure out where he was and how to get home.

XXXIII

The second edition of *Lalo Molfino and the Silent Revolution* was a great success. Cabada printed four thousand copies. Seven reviews appeared in newspapers and magazines in Lima, maybe more, and all of them were favorable, no matter whether the writers were on the left or the right. Toño Azpilcueta's message of unity through creole music seemed to please all sides.

But those articles weren't his only triumph. The rector of the University of San Marcos had called Toño in for a meeting. Smoking like a chimney, the old man had told him that the faculty was considering bringing back the professorship in Peruvian studies. Then he asked him a question that had apparently been eating at him for days on end: "Might you be willing to accept that post? Of course, you'd need to finish your doctorate. But I seem to remember you had a dissertation in hand that you never presented. 'The Street Cries of Lima,' wasn't it?"

Toño nodded, feeling his body slowly ascending into the clouds. He would have to look his dissertation over again, write a conclusion, show it to a few of his professor friends to see if it met with their approval, and find a publisher, if he wanted to achieve any real prestige. He could already see himself teaching classes at San Marcos, and he savored the strange feeling of what was happening to him. He was the talk of the country. The newspapers proved it, the interviewers, the radio programs, the morning talk show he'd been invited onto. When they asked him about commonalities in the Peruvian character, he put on airs, stroking his chin as if he needed to think before responding, even though he knew exactly what he was going to say. The reporters were kind to him, they said he was a man who was modest despite his enormous talent.

"Talent, Matilde, that's what people are saying I have. I keep thinking to myself that at some point I'm going to wake up and find out this is all a dream."

"No, Toño. This is really happening. I don't know if it's good or bad, but it's real."

El Comercio hired him to write four articles summarizing the contents of his book, for which they paid him nearly a thousand *soles*. He joked with Matilde that if his good fortune continued, they'd need a new home. What did she think of Collau's idea of moving to San Miguel? When journalists came to their home in Villa El Salvador, Matilde treated them with a measure of distrust. Toño found it hard to believe that a small book released by a small publisher could have such effects. But Cabada had told him they'd sold four thousand copies. They would likely need to print a third edition and, who knew, perhaps a fourth and fifth.

Looking back at "The Street Cries of Lima," Toño found the draft less disorganized than he'd feared. He was missing a few index cards, but he could recompose them with a bit of patience. He returned to the National Library to work on it. In a matter of months, he was done, and he presented the corrected version at San Marcos. He remembered how angry he'd been when Doctor Morones had informed him the professorship was being canceled due to a lack of students. How lucky he was he hadn't torn his dissertation to pieces then! He spoke with some friends from the department and managed to convince the dean of Arts and Letters to assemble a jury. His defense was deemed excellent, and they recommended publication of the dissertation. If the professorship was revived, there was no better candidate than Toño Azpilcueta. The rector of San Marcos himself, sitting there in his three-piece suit and waving his nicotine-stained fingers around, told him as much at his defense.

At the end of that year, the professorship in Peruvian studies was announced, and Toño received the offer he'd been waiting for. He accepted, surprised at the very respectable salary he was given as well as at the appointment of a research assistant just for him. Whenever he was paid, he immediately turned his check over to Matilde.

His family prospered. One day, a nun from his daughters' school told him, "Mr. Azpilcueta, you must have noticed you're getting quite famous." Yes, he had noticed. He'd received a letter from Adolfo Ibáñez University in Chile offering him a thousand dollars plus travel and hotel expenses to give a single lecture. When he asked if he could bring Matilde, they replied of course, his wife was more than welcome. The invitation terrified him. He had never left Peru; the thought of setting foot on Chilean soil had never occurred to him, and yet now important professors in that country, wishing to know whether his subject might have import in the rest of Latin America, were offering him the opportunity. The thought struck him as so improbable, so absurd, that he grew anxious again. His calves began to burn, irritation spread across his legs. He was about to lose it, he thought, and would soon see rats everywhere. He took a deep breath, closed his eyes to ward off the hallucinations, and lay back for a moment. Once he regained control of himself, he left his house in Villa El Salvador and headed out for San Isidro, where Doctor Quispe's office lay, ready to apologize if he had to, ready to do anything to get the pills he needed. He couldn't travel to Chile without that prescription, he was certain of it: the risk that his nerves would play a nasty trick on him in hostile territory was simply too high.

When he arrived at his stop, after two hours in minibuses, it was night, and he worried Doctor Quispe might no longer be there. He ran the rest of the way, stopping half a block from the building to catch his breath and smooth his jacket. A couple entered, and he walked in with them to avoid having to ring. He took the stairs up to Quispe's office. The nurse looked surprised when he rang the bell. She opened, slightly huffy: she had changed out of her uniform, had her purse slung over her shoulder, and must have been ready to turn off the lights and leave. Recognizing Toño, she let him in, but she warned him that Doctor Quispe was already gone, and added that so far as she knew, Toño hadn't had an appointment that day. Toño told her not to worry, it was better, in fact, if the doctor wasn't there. He just wanted one thing: a prescription for the pills he'd been given once—she must remember them, they were small and blue, and they had worked wonders for him. He just needed the name. The nurse said she had no idea what medicine he was talking about. Besides, she didn't have the authority to issue prescriptions. Toño paused for a moment and thought.

"If I see the bottle, I think I'll recognize it," he said. "Just let me into the doctor's office and I'll figure it out."

He didn't wait for permission before bursting in. She tried to stop him, told him he had no right to be there, but Toño managed to slide past her and shut the door behind him.

"Just wait," he said, "as soon as I find the bottle, I'll be right out." He walked over to Quispe's desk. Those tranquilizers, or whatever they were, that he gave patients who showed up in the grip of anxiety had to be in one of the drawers.

"Get out now! You're not allowed to be in there!" the nurse shouted, pounding on the door.

"I'm coming, lady, don't be like that," Toño said, opening the first drawer.

He didn't find what he was looking for, but what he did find made him forget the medicine he was craving: a copy of *Lalo Molfino and the Silent Revolution*, read from cover to cover by the looks of it. Toño picked it up and opened it at random, finding the margins covered in tiny annotations that reminded him of armies of ants. And that wasn't a coincidence: the entire book was full of underlining and comments. Without thinking, Toño hid the book under his jacket and walked out, startling the nurse, who stepped back to make way for him.

"I apologize, Miss, I didn't mean to frighten you," he said with a slight bow. "I'm leaving now. I don't need the pills, it's fine. You're right—I'll have to come back when the doctor's in, and I won't make such a scene. Again, I'm sorry for disturbing you."

"Doctor Quispe will hear about this. If you're smart, you'll stay away," the nurse replied, still looking alarmed.

Once at the door, Toño bowed to her again. Then he shut it behind him and hurried down the stairs, hoping to leave before the nurse alerted the building's doorman. Outside, he walked to the first streetlamp he could find and leaned against it to read Doctor Quispe's notes. It was hard to make out those minuscule letters, written in a rushed hand, surrounded by exclamation points all over the cheap paper that had been the best Mr. Cabada could afford. As he squinted, the scribbles slowly transformed into legible letters. After ten minutes, Toño slammed the book shut and threw it into the street like a bomb. What he'd read had infuriated him, and his legs, his chest, and his arms were burning. He heard noises and knew that the rats would soon crawl up from the sewer, from the trash bins, from the cracks in the asphalt, hundreds, thousands of them. He took off running, and didn't stop until he managed to wave down the first of the minibuses he would need to take to reach Villa El Salvador.

He tried not to remember what Quispe had written. If he could, he'd forget it all forever. But to spite him, certain phrases kept floating up in his memory. "One more fairy tale fed to Peruvians. Does the author honestly think we'll love each other more thanks to creole music? Seriously?" *Fairy tale,* Toño kept repeating to himself and shaking his head. No, it wasn't a fairy tale, it couldn't be. Elsewhere, surrounded by exclamation points, a note said that the book's thesis was nonsense, a response not to the Peruvian people's needs, but to the wishes of the author, a poor devil who couldn't accept conflict and contradictions. What upset him most was the way the doctor had referred to his choice of subjects—all of them of utmost significance, in Toño's view—as a "pointless, incoherent mass of undeveloped ideas." How could the history and development of Peruvian national character be pointless and incoherent? It was one thing for this doctor to ridicule Toño, another to disdain the essence of Peru itself, the historical, sociological, and cultural ingredients that combined magically to make up the soul of the nation. So Doctor Quispe thought his book was half-baked, a jumble, poorly thought out . . . well, Toño would show him otherwise. He had no qualms about re-editing the work, expanding ideas merely suggested in the present version, adding bolder conjectures and subtler arguments until the book was perfect, seamless, with nothing this Quispe or any other sneering intellectual could deride or dismiss.

Toño worked day and night, giving much thought to the changes his book needed, and on the evening before his departure for Chile, as Matilde packed their bags, he read the fifty pages he had written: a lecture he'd prepared painstakingly, not only for money, not only to impress the Chileans, but because that material would go directly into *Lalo Molfino and the Silent Revolution* as soon as Antenor Cabada informed him that a third edition was needed. In Santiago, a group of professors greeted them at the airport and accompanied them to an elegant hotel. After a dinner out, Toño was told they would be picked up the next morning at ten. He and Matilde slept in a fine bed that night, and bathed and primped in a bathroom fit for a millionaire.

The lecture was a success, and ended in long minutes

of applause. The idea of music as an antidote to conflict and prejudice was a novelty for his audience. A professor asked him if he thought his vision for Peru's future might be relevant for Chile, too, or perhaps for Latin America as a whole. Toño responded cautiously. It wasn't impossible that such a thing could occur, he said, particularly in those societies where popular music had penetrated the middle and upper classes, building a bridge between poor and rich. But it depended, in large measure, on the music itself, its charm, how deeply its roots sank into the hearts of the people across the land. On the afternoon of that unforgettable day, after an interview with *La Tercera*, one of the important local newspapers, the professors once more invited Toño and Matilde to dinner. The conversation was remarkable, erudite, rife with cultural references that left Toño in a daze. Repeatedly, he thought of the question he'd been asked that afternoon. That was what was missing from his book: Latin America as a whole, a vision that spanned the continent and its conflicts—the idea, for example, that his own country's rivalry with Chile might be quelled by a truly popular Latin music. And if such a thing could happen in Latin America, why not in the entire world, to the benefit of humanity as a whole?

Back in Lima, Toño worked harder than ever. Collau would watch him depart with his daughters very early in the morning and return alone very late at night, carrying his suitcase full of notebooks, loose scraps of paper, index cards, and books for his research. They no longer met under the lamppost to talk over the day's events. Toño had informed everyone that his publisher was planning a third edition, and that this time Cabada would invest the whole of his savings in a print run of fifteen thousand copies. That was why Toño was working sixteen-hour days, on top of teaching classes at San Marcos and writing for *El Comercio.* Collau had been curious about his trip to Chile, but all Toño had told him was that the magnificent country to their south had given him what he needed to at last fill the gaps in his book on Lalo Molfino. He looked convinced as he said this, self-assured, and so Collau was happy for him, and proud that his neighborhood could now boast of having a great intellectual in its midst.

Only once, when a letter from Cecilia Barraza arrived for him at the National Library, did Toño interrupt his work. In it, she remarked that she hadn't seen him in a long time, and she invited him for one of their breakfasts at the Bransa, on Friday or Saturday of the following week. Toño read the letter, then returned to his frantic editing.

XXXIV

Toño had a strange feeling as he worked: His critics were right. He had a book in hand, but a disjointed one with blind spots, one that constantly lurched from one subject to the next. It started with Lalo Molfino's life, and that was well executed, he thought, with a natural flow and muted tension, the prose appropriate to the human drama of that master of rhythm. He recreated in terse phrases the night Father Molfino had rescued Lalo, and the later story of his adoption and his schoolboy days in Puerto Etén. And there was the scene of the boys playing soccer, the ball knocked in the air—he liked those passages, and he had reread them several times.

All this was followed by Lalo's discovery of the castoff guitar, perhaps in the same landfill where Father Molfino had found him, and his slow and solitary acquaintance with the instrument. His adolescence came next, and his travels. The story was paced well, the telling clear and precise, with few digressions and a skilled conjuring of the colors and fragrances of Chiclayo. Toño wrote about the performance he'd been to in Abajo el Puente, and the unforgettable patent leather shoes on Lalo Molfino's feet. All of that was profoundly to his liking.

But he felt a certain anxiety as he approached the central

concept of the book: his intimation of the social changes that creole music would bring to Peru. Not daring enough, he told himself; he found his narration too pat, too calibrated to the expectations of his readers, Peruvians rich and poor alike. Starting with La Palizada and their escapades under the incorrigible Karamanduka, moving on to the love story of Toni Lagarde and Lala Solórzano, the Old Guard, Felipe Pinglo Alva—all that was fine, first-rate, even . . . But in what followed, there was something lacking. As the text moved from Lalo Molfino to the history of Peru and Latin America, he sensed that his effort, his ambition, had flagged. A discussion of the past was necessary, but if he wished to go further than all those other writers who had aimed to offer a coherent vision of Peru (and he included here his own master, Hermógenes A. Morones), he would need to try harder, fill all the cracks, make palpable that elusive subject of fraternity, of the essential unity of the Peruvian soul. It was all well and good to talk about the Spanish language, the language of the valses, and as for *huachafería*, with its striking use of diminutives and its imagery, full of pomp and refined sensibilities, he doubted such a thing could exist in English, or in Quechua, for that matter. This expressive force that connected Peru with the rest of the world was only possible in Spanish, and he had to make this clear.

He would need to emphasize more heavily the importance of the Catholic religion and the traces of the Inca Empire in the nation's present. But he also wanted to broaden all these subjects with reflections on the problems he'd become aware of after his trip to Chile. And there were unresolved questions. His book considered bullfighting, for example, but he hadn't asked himself whether that pastime had a place in the society of the future that he envisioned. This was a dilemma for him. He had always admired the bullfighter's art, and had been going to the Plaza de Acho as a spectator since he was a boy; it was his father who had first taken him there during the October Fair, and he had continued attending as an adult, sometimes alone, sometimes with friends and acquaintances from the world of creole music. Those people tended to be connoisseurs of bullfighting as well. This was where he had heard for the first time the silences that seized the bullring in moments of tension, when swordsman and animal seemed to engage in a secret dance, and for a few seconds, or even minutes, the whole world was held in suspension . . . This was the same sensation he felt at certain concerts, when the music seemed to carry away all humdrum worries and anxieties, leaving only a mingling of absolute serenity and utmost concentration.

Toño knew, though, that times were changing, that animal lovers abounded now, that the mistreatment of these creatures had become political, and that aversion to the sport could only grow. Activists deemed bullfighting a barbaric diversion, making a poor beast suffer for the enjoyment of a handful of savages. The lances and barbs came in for the worst criticism, those instruments of torture jabbed into the fighting bull to fatigue it, so that people like Toño could admire the sculptural beauty of the standoff between torero and prey.

Toño wasn't blind to the cruelty of it, but it was an old tradition, one rooted in a mythology of man and bull that stretched back to Europe's earliest days. The god Zeus, transformed into a bull, had seized the princess Europa as his consort, and she had birthed kings who ruled over the lands that bore her name; Europe, in turn, was the mother of the Americas—or the grandmother or great-grandmother, perhaps. And the fighting bull was the most privileged animal in history. Toño had read articles and books describing the careful attention lavished on these beasts in the haciendas where they were raised. Even in Peru, their feed and care were carefully monitored, and veterinarians watched over them in their pens. A dream of his, one he'd probably never fulfill, was to visit one of those haciendas in Mexico or Spain where the grandiose creatures were bred, to observe how the calves grew slowly, under their minders' careful supervision, into the fierce creatures that strode into the ring to show their bravery. All those specimens with their fine horns would vanish if bullfights were prohibited, leaving behind only the portly draft animals familiar from comic strips and cartoons, serenely smelling daisies and chewing their cud in the fields, occasionally flapping their tails to ward off the flies.

All this Toño felt sincerely, but in the depths of his heart and his mind, he told himself at times that the animal rights activists weren't wrong; what roused and sometimes saddened the public in the ring was the blind suffering of a being barely aware, unable to comprehend the trickery the bullfighter and his entourage subjected it to, wounded mortally so the spectators could clap and swoon. But what about all those millions of animals killed in laboratories to make medicines, and the masses of them we never see being slaughtered morning, noon, and night for our nourishment and fancy?

Wedded to his defense of the sport, Toño had examined it thoroughly in his book, with allusions to the traditions of the Andes, like the Yawar Fiesta, in which a drunken condor is tied to the back of a bull in a fusion of the indigenous and Spanish cultures—even there, in the mountains, in the festivities of the poor, the bull was part of folk tradition. And so bullfighting could not be said to be foreign to the Peruvian character. In the new version of his book, he would stress this union—condor and bull, America and Spain—that persisted in the soil of his homeland.

Another question that had vexed him but he'd resigned himself to leaving out was the place of witches and shamans in the cultural revolution Lalo Molfino embodied. One day, Toño had run into Santiago Zanelli, a doctor and a former classmate of his from La Salle, and the two men had gone for a coffee to reminisce about old times. With horror, the doctor had shown him an article from the newspaper *Última Hora* that revealed, among other statistics, that there were three shamans or witches for every doctor in Peru. Was this possible? The idea had shocked Toño, who had devoted some time to researching these people, discovering that indeed, they were like a secret army, dominating Peru from the shadows, especially in the interior provinces. No part of the country was free of them, and yet many Peruvians had no idea of their existence. This was another division in his homeland.

The idea that so many of his countrymen turned to witch doctors to cure their ailments had unsettled Toño for several days. What was most repugnant to him was the apparently widespread belief in Peru that if a witch or shaman passed a guinea pig over a person's naked body, the creature would die as soon as it touched the skin beneath which an infected organ lay. For hours, the patient would have to lie still and allow that filthy cousin of the rat to caress his bare skin. The mere thought of it repelled him.

And all of this took place in cabins or miserable, filthy rooms, because these people with so-called magic powers were poor and had learned their trade from their parents, grandparents, or great-grandparents in lessons passed on in silence. Their work was outside of the law, like drug dealing—and that was another aspect of his homeland that depressed him. Marijuana, pills, cigarettes dipped in who knew what, easy to make, easy to buy, sold cheap to addicts in the street, given away outside the doorways of schools to create future addicts . . . In principle, Toño thought it was people's right to ruin their lives with drugs—to hell with them, was his attitude—but children needed to be cared for until they were old enough to make responsible and realistic decisions about these things.

There was a darkness in his country that these witches and shamans represented. He'd spent hours evoking it in his mind. The police now and then would burst into some basement and discover real or supposed altars to Satan, with decapitated cats or mice, sinks full of human blood, diabolical graffiti on the walls. The devil had thousands of disciples in Peru—and other countries, too—who gathered in these hovels and underground caves where witches and charmers watched over ignorant people devoted to the worship of Lucifer, dancing frenetically, making love in unnatural ways, participating in sodomy and orgies, believing in their benightedness that they were honoring the devil and his minions.

Toño had exalted a hidden, marginal culture in Peru—but was this clandestine world of witchcraft somehow related to it? No, he thought, imagining again his body being rubbed by a filthy guinea pig. What could be more opposed to the *huachafería* he had championed? They were polar opposites. And yet, did these practices and beliefs not have their roots in ancient times, in the period of the Incas or perhaps even earlier, among the Aymara who had preceded them in the region of Puno and Lake Titicaca? The Spanish priests had suppressed their occult beliefs, as had modern medicine in turn, but who knew how much of that arcana had survived past the colonial period, practiced covertly by naïve, ignorant people who had survived into the modern era despite centuries of persecution.

Toño's vision of a revived Peru could not ignore these elements so embedded in the nation's deepest strata, regardless of how much they horrified him. There were many of them, and his thesis would need to incorporate each and every one in a systematic way. That was the path, but where did the line running from the vals to witchcraft and Satanism lie?

These were the tangled questions Toño had attempted to address in the third version of his book. And now it was done, ready, his mission completed, he thought. He sent the new manuscript to his publisher. He was eager to know Cecilia's view of all that had happened to him since *Lalo Molfino and the Silent Revolution* was first published. He would find out on Saturday morning at the Bransa.

XXXV

Cecilia surprised him, after the customary kisses on the cheek, with the declaration that she was tired, and the idea of retirement was tempting her. Toño found this hard to believe.

"But Cecilia, you're still so young. And don't take this the wrong way, but you're more beautiful than you've ever been. Surely you're kidding. What will your legions of admirers all over the world do when they can no longer go see you sing and dance?"

"I told you, I'm exhausted, and it's just not fun the way it used to be," she said. "And the guitarists and the other musicians and the sound guys, they're all such a hassle. What's the point of it all, Toño? I was lucky, I found success even at the beginning of my career, I had the support of the best singers, but it doesn't matter the way it used to. I already have enough money, I've got my own home in Miraflores, and as long as I'm careful, my savings will last me till I die. I'm bored. I'm bored of all these people. I want to rest, see my real friends now and again, see you, just to talk. I need conversation. And why not be honest? I want to watch my soap operas. But tell me about you. You're like a stranger these days . . ."

Toño told her about the big changes in his life. She knew he'd been writing for *El Comercio*, she always read his articles, and she'd heard he was now a professor at San Marcos. But she'd had no idea that they were reading and discussing his work even in Chile.

"I'm pleased that everything's going so well for you, Toño."

Toño observed her new dress, her freshly manicured nails, her hair still immaculate from a trip to the salon. Through her sunglasses, he could see her big eyes, cheerful as always.

"I thought I was coming here to surprise you, Cecilia, and instead, you're the one surprising me," Toño said. "I can't believe you're actually retiring."

"Not yet, Toño, but soon. I'm ready. There are things I want to do—go to museums, look at art. And rest. I deserve it, I think. You reach a point, you know, where nothing has any meaning anymore and you don't know why you keep doing what you're doing."

"I'd never say you don't deserve it, Cecilia. You have a right to enjoy yourself. But think of all your fans, think of me! What are we going to do without you?"

"You'll find someone else to admire, someone you'll look up to even more. It happens with everyone. Think back to all the famous singers this country's had. No one even remembers them anymore. Just Felipe Pinglo Alva, and that's because he died young and of tuberculosis, the 'romantic disease,' they used to call it. Even his admirers are slowly dying off. Tell me about you, though. I see things are going well. Not that it's a justification for you to forget all your old friends."

"Cecilia, I could never forget you. It's just that I haven't had a free second with everything that's been happening.

I'm living a dream. My ideas are reaching people, touching them down deep. They see now that creole music isn't just for amusement, that it has the power to overcome prejudices. It's a miracle. I keep thinking I'm going to wake up and this will all be over, and I'll go back to being a scrounger, writing articles about singers and guitarists and starving or depending on Matilde's washing and sewing for my daily bread."

"It's odd you've never introduced her to me," Cecilia said with a grin. "Maybe now's the time?"

"Matilde would die of jealousy if she saw you," Toño said with a grin of his own, examining Cecilia from head to toe. "She's not like you, she doesn't have your beauty, your elegance. If you insist, I'll introduce you, but I doubt you'll get along. The two of you are very different."

"You know, Doctor Quispe wanted to marry me. He's been chasing after me for years, ever since I started singing. He used to give me necklaces and rings, offered to take me on trips . . . But I've gotten tired of him, too. I did hear you skipped your therapy with him, then returned one night and rummaged around in his desk for pills. I convinced him not to press charges. What happened that day? Have you been having more of your attacks or whatever you'd call them?"

Before Toño could answer, Antenor Cabada approached their table frantically.

"I knew you'd show up here sooner or later, Toño," he said, adjusting his glasses as he prepared to launch into a tirade. "Have you lost your mind? Do you actually expect me to publish a new edition with more than a hundred new pages? You started off talking about a guitarist from Puerto Etén, then it was Peru, now it's bullfights and witches and drugs and the fate of Latin America and all of humanity. You've lost me. You had a successful book, you already revised it once and made it almost unreadable, but this time, you've gone beyond the pale. Are you trying to bankrupt me? Do you want to burn through all your newfound prestige?"

Toño serenely introduced Cabada to Cecilia Barraza and invited him to sit, telling him to calm down as he pulled out a chair for him. "What I've given you," he began, "is a book without a single crack in it. I've anticipated every possible objection to my assertions, and now no one, absolutely no one in the entire world, can cast doubt on them."

"I invested all of my savings in this new edition, I even had to take out a loan," Cabada protested. "Do you not realize the printer is going to charge me for this new material? You've turned this thing into a doorstop, a labyrinth. How do you expect readers to find their way through it?"

Glancing at Cecilia, Toño said wryly, "Publishers. Always putting cash before knowledge."

She defended Toño: "Mr. Cabada, the book's already successful. Undoubtedly what Toño's added will only improve it. No one would idly destroy something they've worked so hard on. Toño's always had a clear sense of what he's doing. If he didn't, he wouldn't have made it this far. They're even talking about him in Chile. Whatever the printer's asking for, I'll bet it will be the best investment you've ever made."

Toño could have kissed her when he saw Cabada's expression change, his hostility fade away. He seemed to take Cecilia's words to heart.

"I hope God's listening to you," he said. "And it's a pleasure meeting you, by the way. I apologize for my bad manners."

"Toño should be an example to all the scholars out there; no one is more passionate than he is," Cecilia went on. "Maybe he's a perfectionist, but can you really hold that against him? I'd think you'd do better to congratulate him for it. Imagine a writer simply not caring about their book, not wanting to make it better. Trust me, the new edition will be a success."

"Of course, ma'am," Cabada said, somewhat cowed. "I'm sure you're right. After all, Toño's the writer—I suppose he knows his subject. He'll be able to defend his conclusions. You have to understand, though, I'm gambling my entire company here. I suppose I can be forgiven for being a little nervous. Still, I shouldn't have accosted you like this. I'll leave you be. Again, my apologies."

Toño waited for Cabada to leave before thanking Cecilia for her intervention. He smiled with relief.

"I'm telling the truth, though, Toño," she said. "You talk about your ideas with such conviction, even I wind up believing them. It's impossible not to, and at the very least, we should be happy we finally have someone in this country proposing something original, giving people something to debate. Your book is taking a stand for creole music—that's going to be your legacy."

Knowing that if these compliments continued, he'd be unable to contain himself and would once again confess his love for her, Toño invented an excuse to leave. He had more ideas—how could it be otherwise?—and perhaps there was still time to find room for them in the third edition. If not, then in the fourth.

XXXVI

What would old Professor Morones have said about Toño's theory that music would transform Peruvian society from the ground up? Nothing, probably. He rarely spoke when something wasn't to his liking. He'd have kept silent, cleared his throat, and quickly changed the subject. Morones had been a respectable man who lived modestly in Breña, spending every cent he made at San Marcos on books, journals, and music. Toño had known him well, and had been to his home many times, and he imagined that if his former instructor were alive, he would have added his voice to the small chorus of professors who had begun to denounce his book as nonsense.

This thought first occurred to him after he received notice of a meeting to take place at the university. The end of the year was approaching, and the rector wished to discuss the curriculum. Toño knew this would give his colleagues the opportunity to object to his position as chair of Peruvian studies. He'd begun with seventeen students; their numbers had dwindled to four, but he didn't mind, because there were always others who showed up to hear the music he played in class. These drop-ins nearly filled the room and even contributed to the discussion. But they didn't register for the course, not even the ones studying Peruvian literature.

Toño was nervous, and lacked the energy to prepare his classes. All he could think about was the professors mounting a conspiracy with the rector to eliminate his post. He didn't understand why more students hadn't signed up, or why the latest reviews of his book, all contemptuous, had become the talk of the university hallways. People who had found his assertions interesting at first now said they were incomprehensible *huachafería*, the kind of tripe you find in self-help books. And Cabada had left a letter for him at the Bransa, saying they had to talk immediately. He'd had to raise the price of the new edition by three *soles*, and that had dissuaded buyers in the provinces. Cabada had paid extra to have the book distributed as quickly as possible, and now all the copies were being returned, often in lamentable condition. He'd hoped to salvage the situation with a television interview he'd managed to set up through a friend, but Toño had been impossible to reach, so they'd never agreed on a date. That was a missed opportunity to attract more readers to what Cabada called "this preposterous third edition." He was on the verge of bankruptcy, "but it's not just me, it's you, my friend," the letter had continued, "because you're the one most responsible for this, with your absurd delusions of grandeur. My only fault was being too stupid to bring you back down to earth." Cabada warned he wasn't about to go down alone, he would take Toño to court if he had to. His complaints and reproaches continued, but after a certain point, Toño stopped reading them. He didn't understand what was happening. With every revision, he'd made his book stronger, broadened its range. This time, he'd left nothing out. It was destined to be a success in Peru and across Latin America. It was just a matter of time with a book that ambitious, one that addressed all the doubts that plagued the human heart . . .

The meeting fell toward the end of final exams. Toño had generally attended such affairs with reluctance, to fulfill an obligation, without listening closely to what the people gathered had to say. They'd never interested him, but this morning was obviously different. It opened with complaints and petitions, mostly from professors who wanted their budgets increased; those whose classes were crowded demanded more assistants to help with practicums. Toño hoped they would get bogged down in these debates and the fate of his own post would be forgotten.

But the rector with the nicotine-stained fingers hadn't forgotten the matter, and as things wound to a close, he brought up Toño, ringing a tiny bell to get the attendees' attention.

"Now we must turn to a delicate issue," he began. "Naturally, I'm referring to Peruvian studies. You all are aware this has been a problem area for us ever since we reinstated the professorship. The department is overseen by a distinguished chair, as you all know. I am referring, of course, to Doctor Toño Azpilcueta."

Here it comes, Toño thought, feeling his heart skip a beat. He had devised all sorts of arguments in his defense, but he barely had a chance to utter them. He had planned to fight tooth and nail to save his professorship. But the rector's argument was numerical, and numbers were something he couldn't argue with.

"We had seventeen students signed up when we brought

the department back," the rector said, glancing through his papers, then continuing casually, "and now we have only four. I understand that there are many people auditing the classes, but those don't count. You must know, a department survives on active enrollments, not auditors."

Toño raised his hand and the rector ceded the floor. Toño was gripped by the same feeling he had experienced the night he had presented his book to a nearly empty auditorium at the Ministry of Education. The situation was more or less the same. Already, the professors were filing out, in a hurry to catch their buses home for lunch.

He spoke with enthusiasm, giving every possible reason why the Peruvian Studies department should remain, but the counterargument was simply too strong. What was the point of it all, with so few students? It simply didn't make sense. The rector put the professorship's survival to a vote, and Toño was defeated by a crushing majority. The rector concluded with a few kind words about Professor Azpilcueta and his struggle to discharge his responsibilities with the highest academic rigor, which he had done consummately, it must be acknowledged; and he ended with a reference to unfortunate economic factors that simply couldn't be ignored. When he was about to send everyone on their way, Toño asked if he could speak again.

"We can dispense with the song and dance intended to cover up what's really happening here, esteemed colleagues, or rather, ex-colleagues," Toño said solemnly, in a nasal tone. "Why try to sweep it under the rug? This isn't a concession to economic necessities. That's rhetoric, a smoke screen, but the truth, the reality, is evident. What is it, then? Allow me to tell you in one simple word, one all of you are surely familiar with. A plot! In this beloved university, but not only here, in all of Peru, there is a conspiracy against me. With great shame, I must charge my colleagues, my ex-colleagues, with resentment, with a refusal to allow my ideas to triumph here and across our borders. Perhaps you're unaware that the man before you is read in Chile, my friends? And here, I have captivated readers from the most refined to those who barely ever pick up a book. But these men and women of the provinces feel creole music in their hearts and know that it is the beginning of the solution to all our problems. The hostility of intellectuals to my ideas can only mean one thing: that they want Peru divided, torn by rivalries! They want us to remain strangers to each other. And they know that if I fail, my project will fail—the project of bringing Peruvians together in peaceful brotherhood. There is a name for such people who prefer corruption to fraternity. Do you know what it is? Shall I tell you? Rats!"

"Professor Azpilcueta!" the rector interrupted him, striking his desk. "I will not allow you to insult the faculty of this university."

"Rats!" Toño shouted again.

"This meeting is adjourned," the rector said above the murmurs filling the hall.

Those professors who remained then stood and walked toward the exit, looking reproachfully at Toño, who was on his feet, shouting "Rats!" over and over. The rage and the vehemence were gone: now his voice was broken, scared. One of the professors noticed his eyes were open wide, as though from shock, and she walked over and asked if he was all right. She heard Toño mumbling to himself, "Rats, rats . . ." Sensing her presence, Toño grabbed her arm the way a castaway grasps at a life preserver on the open sea. "Rats," he whispered to her, "rats . . . rats . . ." He was shaking. The professor cupped his face and looked him in the eyes, but he couldn't focus—his pupils were dilated, and he seemed unaware of his surroundings. She shouted for help. Several professors, the rector among them, carried Toño to the university infirmary. An hour later, the students were having lunch in the cafeteria, Lima quieted down, as it always did at midday, and an ambulance arrived to take Toño away.

XXXVII

In the distance, two figures, small at first, advance through the clear morning. As they approach Miraflores Central Park, they grow until at last they are normal sized. The Avenida Larco is empty. Bags and loose paper dot the streets. A reflection in the distance, around Salazar Park, hints at the imminent sunrise. Soon, farther off, at the foot of the hill, the glimmer of the sea will be visible. Thankfully, the day in store will be warm and bright.

The two people have risen early. The man is wearing a green jacket. His shirt collar sticks out of it, pastel yellow with a pattern of various colors. A baseball cap conceals part of his face. The woman is shorter than he, elegant in a thin summer dress and moccasins, hair neat, as though she had prepared for the occasion carefully upon rising. It is eight o'clock at the latest.

Slowly they approach the little square at the center of Miraflores, talking. Around them are the city hall, the church, the park, the benches under the trees, and the damp grass recently cut by the gardeners who are beginning their day's work.

"Miraflores seems so different," Toño says, looking all about. "I haven't been here in ages. Certainly not at this hour."

"It's full of shops now, and there's so much traffic," Cecilia Barraza says. "It's not as nice as it used to be. Fortunately my apartment's on a high floor, so I don't really notice. Look there, and there, all those are shops, every kind you can imagine. You can buy anything here, from a car to a thimble. They've destroyed the neighborhood. It used to be nice, walking around here. I remember when I was little, my father would bring us here, holding our hands, and all you saw in the park were street peddlers. Even in the nineties, once the terrorist attacks were over, it was a nice place for a stroll. Now, though, look at it, it's just awful."

"Things change," Toño remarks with an exaggerated grimace. "But it's true, you can't say these shops have added to Miraflores's charm."

"They're not nice, like the elegant stores in San Isidro. We've gone down-market, Toño. You can even buy lottery tickets here."

"You can't complain, though, Cecilia. Your view from up there must be stunning. You can probably hear the roar of the sea in every room."

"It's not bad up there on the fourth floor. I would have had you in, but it's a mess. The furniture and carpets are new though, and I have keepsakes and photos everywhere. It's looking nice. When it's ready, I'll have you over for tea, as your friends Toni and Lala used to do, may they rest in peace."

"Toni Lagarde and Lala Solórzano," Toño says nostalgically, as though evoking figures of legend. "No one outlasts time, but they had many good years. You should have seen how they lived. In a hovel in Breña, happy as could be."

"You've talked about them so much, and about Lala's jam, that I decided to learn how to make it. You'll have to come over for some one day, Toño, it'll surprise you, you'll see."

"You making jam, Cecilia? Surely not. But I swear, if it's anything like Lala's, you'll earn yourself a kiss."

"On the cheek," Cecilia responds coyly, "or on the hand. Not on the lips."

"I know, Cecilia," Toño says. "I know, no kisses on the lips. I would never dare try such a thing again. We're just friends, and even that is a miracle to me. I've thought of you a lot, but I began to doubt I'd really known you. The doctors told me I was making it up, and in the end, I believed them. A person like me being friends with the great Cecilia Barraza—they couldn't imagine that was really true."

"Don't say that," Cecilia says, slapping his arm. "You're the incomparable Toño Azpilcueta, the greatest expert in creole music in Peru, the author of . . ."

"Don't bring it up, please," Toño interrupts her.

They walk past the façade of the church, take a stroll through the gardens. The garbage men sweep up the empty beer cans and soft drink bottles, the cigarette butts and matches, and where someone has spit up phlegm, they spray a little water before scrubbing. The park starts to look better, brighter as they do their work.

"It's pretty here at dawn, especially in the summer," Toño says. "You know what time I got up to make it here? Just before six. Is there somewhere to have breakfast nearby? To be honest with you, I'm dying of hunger."

"Of course," Cecilia responds. "La Tiendecita Blanca.

They open early. And since it's Sunday, they'll have lady fingers you can dip in your tea. Or hot chocolate, if it doesn't bother your stomach."

"That sounds delightful," Toño tells her with a smile. "Hot chocolate and . . . lady fingers, you said?"

"I did. They're to die for, I'll have a few myself. I often come here just to get them. There's nowhere else in Lima that does them right: hot, fresh out of the oven, you'll see. They're Swiss originally, I believe. Anyway, the owners of the café are. Let's go there."

"You know, Cecilia, this is the first time you and I have met in Miraflores. Maybe this is it for the Bransa?"

"It's too far," she complains. "Even in a taxi, it took me half an hour to get there. I didn't care for the clientele, either. Here, we can be by ourselves and talk."

"I'm glad I came then. It's been ages since I've seen you," Toño muses.

"I know. I had started to think perhaps we were drifting apart. That our friendship wasn't what it had been. At least I never wondered whether you'd existed, though!"

"I was busy. My finances were in terrible shape; I've been writing articles about music morning, noon, and night. But you were and always have been my closest friend. And you always will be. Don't forget it."

"I hope you're right, Toño. Flings and lovers come and go, but friends stay the same, and they're always there for you."

"Are you sure this place will be open?"

"Yes, they open at the crack of dawn for this group of old men that goes there to eat and play chess. We'll be fine."

"Be careful with that term 'old men,' Cecilia. You sound disrespectful. And you and I aren't so young anymore, either."

"It's true," she muses with a smile. "The years pass and the gray hairs keep sprouting, no matter how I cover them up. I'll leave the old men in peace, then, Toño. That's a promise."

Crossing the park, they reach the corner of the Avenida Ricardo Palma and find La Tiendecita Blanca open, just as Cecilia has promised. She chides him: "I told you so!" A moment later, the two are sitting across from each other at a table on the terrace, ordering their lady fingers and their two cups of freshly made hot chocolate—extra hot.

"This will probably do a number on me," Cecilia says, "but since it's the first time you've come to have breakfast with me in Miraflores, I'm going to indulge myself."

Toño nods and looks out at the big buildings rising up along the Avenida José Pardo, feeling a kind of surprise that this, too, is the city where he lives.

"How have you been all this time?" Cecilia asks, her voice changing, her expression suddenly serious. "Are you getting used to your new situation?"

"I'm resigned. I think that's the best way to put it," Toño responds. "The music magazines pay less than they used to for my reviews. They're probably right to, because I probably write worse than before. I'm not ashamed, or not too ashamed, to say I'm only keeping my head above water thanks to Matilde. It's more or less always been that way, anyhow. She and two other women from the neighborhood started a shop doing alterations and such. The girls graduated high school, they're in college now. They're doing well. They take good care of me. Despite everything, we're getting by."

"Are you still living in Villa El Salvador?"

"No, we moved to San Miguel with the help of my friend Collau. He opened a Chinese place, a big one, a few years back. He lends me a hand when he can. In return, I help with the cleaning. He's a good guy, he's always been kind to us."

"I'm pleased to hear about your daughters," Cecilia says, sounding sincere. "Women should go to school, get a degree, give men a run for their money. A profession, that's the secret. Here in Peru, women have been second-class citizens since the Incas. Enough is enough."

Toño nods to satisfy her and keeps to himself his frustrations with women in modern Peru, who are getting cheekier and more defiant by the day, he thinks.

"I got lucky as far as women go," Toño says. "I've always had the best ones close to me. Like you, Cecilia."

"You know me, Toño. If you ever need help, I'm here. I'm sure Doctor Quispe would help you out, too, if you needed him."

"Yes, Doctor Quispe," Toño muses, the memory now vague in his mind. "What a pleasure it was, my brief episode as his patient."

"You may not have liked him, Toño, but he's good, a professional."

"I know, I know, a wonderful man," he interrupts. "Classy, like you. The kind of man who could win your heart."

Cecilia hides her face behind her mug of hot chocolate

as she slowly chews her pastry. After a moment, she remarks, "You have to admit, this is better than those buns you used to gobble down at the Bransa."

"No doubt. Exquisite," he responds.

"Toño, you're acting strange now, I'd almost prefer you get angry and say Doctor Quispe's a quack," Cecilia confesses, pushing her cup and her plate aside.

"God forbid I say such a thing about a master of the healing arts."

"Oh, please, Toño," she complains. "Fine. Let's just say he's a quack, then. He didn't help you, he wouldn't even give you the pills when you needed them."

"They wouldn't have done much," Toño admits.

"Are you sure? What about that day in San Marcos? Maybe if you'd had them, you wouldn't have . . ." She wavers for a moment. "What exactly was it that happened there, Toño?"

"You know perfectly well what happened."

"You're better now, though! Why don't you try to go back to San Marcos? Really fight for the professorship. The Toño I knew was a man of conviction. You had so much faith in everything you said," she asserts softly.

"I was confused. Those were years of confusion. Matilde has taught me to live with my feet on the ground. I have to be thankful to her." Toño narrows his eyes.

"What about your ideas? Your projects?"

"They're gone. And I'm better off for it."

"You no longer believe that creole music will bring us together?" Cecilia seems almost crestfallen as she asks. "You know, I always loved singing and making people happy, but it wasn't until I heard you that I felt important and proud of what I did. I never sang with the same passion and enthusiasm as I did after meeting you at the Bransa and talking to you about Lalo Molfino and your book."

"It's been forever since I heard you sing," Toño tells her, ignoring her remarks about him. "It would make me happy, you know, if you'd sing me one of your famous songs."

"Fine, but I need you to tell me something. I need you to tell me you were right. That creole music isn't just entertainment. I could have retired years ago, I nearly did, but I believed you, you made me see that music was so much more important than I'd imagined. Now I'm questioning myself. And I don't want to. Tell me not to, Toño. Convince me."

"Who am I to tell you what to do?" Toño's voice is full of regret.

"You're the author of . . ."

"I told you, no. I don't want to talk about that. I got wrapped up in my fantasies, and it's only thanks to Matilde, the one person who never let her imagination deceive her, that I'm where I am, more or less happy, with a prosperous and intact family."

"So that's it? That's your life now? Your routines, filling your stomach, the end?" Cecilia seems disillusioned.

"I don't itch anymore. I'm not being stalked by rats. That means something."

"I'd almost rather see you the other way, shirt rolled up, scratching yourself all over like a maniac. What do the rats matter, Toño? Let them come back if your passion for music returns with them."

Toño takes a sip from his cup and realizes his hot chocolate has gone cold. He looks at the clotted cream floating on the surface.

"Will you sing for me, Cecilia? Softly, so only I can hear it."

Instead of responding, she asks, "Do you no longer believe this country will solve its problems one day, Toño?"

"Sure. Eventually, maybe. But you and I won't see it, Cecilia. These are big issues, and they don't have simple solutions."

Cecilia smiles, trying to wish away the black clouds threatening their good cheer. "Well, we'll work things out. No need for despair. One of these days, they'll discover some new mineral that can only be found in Peru. Then we'll all be rich. See how easy it will be?"

Toño laughs. "Easy indeed. Don't ever lose your optimism, Cecilia. It suits you."

"Careful with the compliments, Toño. Remember, we're just good friends. And promise me you won't stay away for so long next time."

"Don't worry," Toño tells her. "It's been a pleasure seeing you. You're holding up well. Always young, always gorgeous. I'll call you at least every two weeks so we can go on having our little breakfasts together."

"But in Miraflores, right? You know I hate going downtown. People recognize me, they ask for autographs. Please, let's stick to Miraflores."

Toño nods. "Miraflores it is."

He stands to call over the waiter, and Cecilia notices as a small notebook falls out of his back pocket.

"You dropped something, Toño," she tells him mischievously. "Might I ask what you're writing?"

"Nothing," he says.

Cecilia smirks, looking him straight in the eye. "If you

tell me, I'll sing a little song in your ear, whichever one you like, just for you."

"It's just more of my nonsense, Cecilia. I can't tell you yet, it's not far enough along. If it goes anywhere, I promise you'll be the first to know. My first reader. And if everything turns out well, I'll dedicate the book to you."

They ask for the check. As always, Cecilia insists on paying. They argue a bit, but Toño gives in. "You're the rich one," he concedes. They leave La Tiendecita Blanca and walk down the Avenida Larco, where the day is showing signs of beginning. Men and women stroll past, vendors look for a place on the sidewalk, the shops are opening and putting their goods on display. The sun shines as Toño and Cecilia talk, keeping a prudent distance from one another, though now and then, they come closer, and she seems to whisper something in his ear. When they used to have breakfast on the Plaza de Armas, Toño would walk her to her taxi. In this new stage, he walks her home before catching bus after bus until he finally arrives back in San Miguel, the place he now calls home.

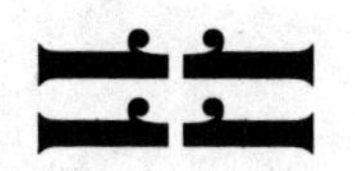

The first draft of this novel was completed in Madrid on April 27, 2022, and corrected, with minor changes, from May to December of that same year. Afterward, I traveled to the north of Peru to visit Chiclayo and Puerto Etén. This journey was fruitful, and with it, I have managed to bring this work to completion. Now, I would like to write an essay about Jean-Paul Sartre, who was my master when I was a young man. That will be the last thing I will ever write.

—Mario Vargas Llosa

TRANSLATOR'S NOTE

My preference is, in general, not to furnish my translations with notes; it feels a bit like loading the dice. But Mario Vargas Llosa's *I Give You My Silence* is a book difficult even for Spanish speakers reading the original who are unfamiliar with the music and popular culture of Peru, and I trust a few brief remarks will ease the reader's way in English. We can begin with the word "creole" (*criollo* in Spanish). By 1580, according to the soldier poet Garcilaso de la Vega, it was an established term (likely derived from the Portuguese *crioulo*) for the offspring of Spaniards or of Africans born in the Americas rather than their native country. Over the succeeding centuries, it would acquire numerous cultural and ethnic meanings in different countries, apart from the linguistic one of a former pidgin codified into a language proper.

Very early in the colonial Americas, there arose conflicts between the "white" creole Spanish and their nominal compatriots in the metropole (I place the term "white" in quotation marks because the Spanish understanding of race was both more permeable and more discriminating than its North American counterpart; interested readers may turn to Magnus Mörner's amenable book, *Race Mixture in the History of Latin America*). The consolidation of continental and territorial notions of identity, which worked to the detriment of Spanish dominion in the Americas, necessarily altered the understanding of what it meant to be a creole, and with the collapse of the Spanish Empire in the early nineteenth century, the "creole" idea evolved in several independent directions in the newly formed nations. In Peru, its racial connotations diminished with respect to cultural ones that emphasized the roguishness, pride, and vivacity of the creole music of the coast. In the present novel, Vargas Llosa declares himself an enemy of racism and chauvinism and takes the inextricable mix of influences—African, indigenous, and Spanish—that contribute to Spanish popular culture as well as to the bloodlines of Peruvian people as an emblem for a kind of folk cosmopolitanism, a cosmopolitanism based not on the sophisticated habits of elites but on the mutual admiration of difference among neighbors, which he sees as essential to the redemption of humanity as a whole.

Schopenhauer called music inexpressible; Miles Davis said, "If you have to ask, you'll never know"; and so I won't exasperate readers by attempting to explain the Peruvian *vals*, the object of Vargas Llosa's affections in this book and one of its major themes. I will simply say that the word *vals* is cognate with *waltz*, and that the Peruvian or creole version (both terms are used interchangeably) was originally an adaptation of the European waltz to colonial tastes. Vargas Llosa offers his own interpretation of the music and its history here. The French scholar Gérard Borras has written an exhaustive work on the subject, *Lima, el vals y la canción criolla (1900–1936)*, which Vargas Llosa cites; for those who do not read Spanish, or who lack the patience to peruse its eight hundred–plus pages, most of its greatest practitioners are amply represented on YouTube, and the same is true of the dances mentioned here throughout.

What I have called "alleyways"—the *callejones* of Lima—are not alleys in the English sense. They are narrow streets, often covered, lined with humble dwellings, and their outlines date back to colonial times, when they housed one- or two-story dwellings of adobe or other rough materials, with passageways of pounded earth connecting one home to another. In them was long preserved the traditional union of home and business, with men and women emerging at midday or evening to sell foods or other goods in their doorways. The unique culture and ways of life that developed in them are the theme of Jimmy Valdivieso's documentary *Mi Barrios Altos Querido.*

Huachafería is mentioned in an earlier Vargas Llosa novel, *The Bad Girl*. To translate it here would have been foolish, as it is one of the central themes of the present text, and the author devotes many pages to its contradictions, connotations, nuances, and possible origins. I will simply inform readers here that dictionaries typically define it as "pretension."

Vargas Llosa finished this novel just shy of three years before his death in April 2025. In the brief afterword, he states that it was to be his last. How clear this was to him is now evident, as the Spanish newspaper *El País* recently revealed he was diagnosed with a terminal illness in 2020. He spent his last months in Peru, and there are photos of him in several of the settings for this novel, as well as one of him standing in front of the now-long-closed bar La Catedral of *Conversation in the Cathedral* fame, which is quite moving when compared to a black-and-white image of him there in the place's heyday in the 1960s. He died among family, among the familiar places he pays homage to in *I Give You My Silence*, and now I will be silent as well, leaving the last word to his son Álvaro, who spoke directly to his father in a funeral address, recounting a rushed transcontinental flight to say goodbye. "I was traveling to bring this dialogue to a conclusion, forever. You received me with a burst of laughter as though to say: you're wrong, this dialogue will continue, just in a different form."

—Adrian Nathan West

A NOTE ABOUT THE AUTHOR

Mario Vargas Llosa (1936–2025) was awarded the Nobel Prize in Literature "for his cartography of structures of power and his trenchant images of the individual's resistance, revolt, and defeat." He also received the Miguel de Cervantes Prize, the Spanish-speaking world's most distinguished literary honor. His many works include *The Feast of the Goat*, *In Praise of the Stepmother*, and *Aunt Julia and the Scriptwriter*, all published by Farrar, Straus and Giroux.

A NOTE ABOUT THE TRANSLATOR

Adrian Nathan West is a novelist, an essayist, and a translator who lives between the United States and Spain. His work has appeared in *The New York Review of Books*, *The Times Literary Supplement*, the *London Review of Books*, *The Baffler*, and many other publications. He is the author of *The Aesthetics of Degradation* and the novel *My Father's Diet*.